THE SECOND
MRS. GIACONDA

THE SECOND
MRS. GIACONDA

By

E. L. KONIGSBURG

ALADDIN BOOKS
MACMILLAN PUBLISHING COMPANY
NEW YORK

COLLIER MACMILLAN CANADA
TORONTO
MAXWELL MACMILLAN INTERNATIONAL PUBLISHING GROUP
NEW YORK   OXFORD   SINGAPORE   SYDNEY

ALADDIN BOOKS
MACMILLAN PUBLISHING COMPANY
866 THIRD AVENUE
NEW YORK, NY 10022

COLLIER MACMILLAN CANADA, INC.
1200 EGLINTON AVENUE EAST
SUITE 200
DON MILLS, ONTARIO M3C 3N1
FIRST ALADDIN BOOKS EDITION 1981
PRINTED IN THE UNITED STATES OF AMERICA
5 7 9 10 8 6 4

FRONTISPIECE: LA JOCONDE;
COURTESY ALINARI—ART REFERENCE BUREAU

ISBN 0-689-70450-X

FIRST AND LAST
for Paul, Laurie and Ross

THE SECOND
MRS. GIACONDA

WHY, PEOPLE ASK, why did Leonardo da Vinci choose to paint the portrait of the second wife of an unimportant Florentine merchant when dukes and duchesses all over Italy and the King of France as well, were all begging for a portrait by his hand? Why, they ask, why?

The answer to that lies with Salai.

Lies with Salai is a fitting expression, for Salai was a liar. Gian Giacomo de' Caprotti, called Salai, was also a thief. Leonardo himself says so. In his notebooks, written in that strange backward hand of his, he calls him, *liar, thief, mule-head, glutton.*

Leonardo's first mention of Salai is this:

Giacomo came to live with me on St. Mary Magdalene's Day, 1490, aged 10 years. The second day I had two shirts cut out for him, a pair of hose and a jerkin. . . .

Next we find this:

ITEM: On the 26th of January following, I being in the house of Messer Galeazzo da San Severino, was arranging the festival, and certain footmen having undressed to try on some costumes for the said festival, Giacomo went to the purse of one of them which lay on the bed with other clothes, and took out such money as was in it.

And then this:

. . . this Giacomo stole the Turkish hide and sold it to a cobbler for 20 soldi with which money, by his own confession he bought anise comfits.

Later references to Salai cease to mention his thievery, but he continues to be listed in Leonardo's household accounts. And then there is this:

I had 30 scudi; 13 I lent to Salai to make up his sister's dowry, and 17 I have left.

Finally, Salai is mentioned in Leonardo's will:

ITEM: I, Leonardo da Vinci, give and bequeath henceforth forever to Salai my servant one-half of my garden which is outside the walls of Milan; in the garden aforesaid Salai has built and constructed a house which shall be and remain henceforth in all perpetuity the property of the said Salai, his heirs and successors; and this is for the good and kind services which the said Salai, my servant, has done me in past time until now.

Why, people ask, why did Leonardo da Vinci put up with this liar, this thief, this Salai? Why for so long? Why did he help pay for his sister's dowry, and why did he remember him in his will?

Why?

Those answers lie in these pages.

IT WAS HOT in Milan that day in July. Salai could think of nothing but the heat and his discomfort in it. He wandered over toward the castle. People coming from and going into a castle always looked cool to him. The rich seemed to walk in a private breeze. But today their looks did nothing for Salai except make him feel even hotter by comparison. He could not be rich, so he could not be cool. He would have to solve the problem of the heat the poor man's way: by thinking of something else. He thought about sweet things to eat. As soon as he had some money, he would buy some anise comfits and eating those would make him feel cool.

Not having money was not the same kind of problem as not being rich; not having money was only temporary.

Salai walked closer and closer to the castle until he spotted two gentlemen leaving. He quickly walked in their direction and bumped into one of them, scurrying off, apologizing and continuing to walk rapidly as if he had somewhere to go. He did not get far. Someone grabbed him from behind, pulling his head back, back over his shoulders, causing Salai to look up, up and further up into the eyes, the fiercely bright eyes, of the man who had grabbed him. The man seemed as tall as Heaven itself, and the man had a beard that sparkled almost as much as his eyes. Only on the wall painting in his church had Salai ever seen eyes like that and a beard like that and a coat like that, as tall and as blue as the Milan summer skies. He shrugged. God at last had caught up with him.

"Let go of that which you have taken," the God-man commanded.

Salai dropped the wallet.

"Now, drop your knife," the God-man said.

"That would blunt it," Salai answered.

"Then give it to me," the God-man said. He held out his hand, a large, immaculate left hand, and Salai placed his knife in it.

The other fellow said, "I swear, Leonardo, I did not know that my wallet had been cut. Is there nothing too quick for you to see?"

8

The God-man laughed. He spun the boy around and said, "Why did you steal this man's purse?"

"I stole nothing," Salai replied. "My knife only accidentally rubbed the thong when I bumped into him. The purse fell into my hands. The thong must have a worn spot."

The man to whom the purse belonged tossed it up in the air. "Well, Leonardo," he said, "a poor excuse has the same mother as a good one; both are born of desperation." He then turned to Salai and asked, "Young man, do you have any idea who it is that caught you?"

"Is he God, sir?" Salai asked.

The man laughed. "No, he is not God; he is one of God's finest inventions."

"Oh," Salai said. "Does that mean that he is of the church?"

"No."

"Is he part of the duke's family?"

"No, no, no," the man said. He then addressed his friend in the long blue robe. "I would have him hanged, not for snatching my purse but for not knowing who you are." He looked again at Salai and said, "The gentleman who had you by the back of your hair is Leonardo da Vinci, the greatest artist, the greatest mind, the greatest engineer at the court of Milan, and that makes him the greatest in the world."

Salai blinked. "If he is not God, and he is not part of the

church nor is he part of the duke's family, then I shall stick to my tale: your purse was cut by accident."

The man laughed. "Let's let him go, Leonardo. He will not be out of trouble for long. Someone else can be bothered with having him hanged."

Leonardo rubbed his hand over Salai's head and took one of the boy's curls between his forefinger and thumb. "What a pity," he said, "that the dirt keeps the sunshine out of these locks. Were they to be washed, Jason himself would mistake them for the Golden Fleece."

Salai had no idea who Jason was, but he knew that the man called Leonardo was saying something kind. He smiled at him.

"What were you going to do with the purse you cut?"

"I cut no purse, sir. My knife accidentally rubbed a worn place in the thong."

Leonardo reached into his own wallet and took from it a single silver coin. He handed it to the boy. "Now son," he said, "this is for you. What will you do with it?"

"Oh, sir," Salai said, "You are most generous." He made a little bow. "You are indeed one of God's finest inventions. With this coin I can buy my sainted father enough leather for a pair of boots."

"Let us go and meet this sainted father of yours," Leonardo said. He then turned to the other fellow and tossed him his wallet. "Go," he said. "I will meet you later at the studio."

They walked through the streets of Milan, the tall, handsome man with the brightness of God in his eyes, and the small street urchin, the young thief, Salai. The boy skipped along, thinking only of the walk, having forgotten his narrow escape from the law and not thinking of the encounter he would soon have with his father.

"That is my father's place," Salai said, pointing.

Leonardo laughed, the sounds seeming to push down inside him instead of puffing out into the air. The boy looked at him, took a reading and joined in the laughter. "Oh!" Leonardo exclaimed. "Your tongue is even quicker than your hand. Your father is a bootmaker. I thought that my coin would be shodding a poor beggar, but I see now that buying enough leather for a pair of boots would only be helping your father to turn a profit." He rubbed his forehead with his hand and said, "Come, boy, there is something I want to talk over with your father, your sainted father, as you call him."

When Leonardo emerged from his talk, he asked Salai, "How would you like to cease being the son of a bootmaker and start being the apprentice of Leonardo da Vinci?"

"Will I have a blue shirt, sir?"

"Yes."

"When?"

"Soon."

"Will I still be Salai, sir?"

"You will always be Salai."

"Then it will be fine with me."

Salai's father could not afford the apprentice fee, so Leonardo took him without. But Salai was not impressed. Having for a brief moment thought that God had him by the back of his hair, it was something of a disappointment to learn that it was only Leonardo da Vinci.

SALAI was the youngest apprentice in Leonardo's studio. He was expected to do all the small chores that no one else wanted to do. He had about him a cheerful willingness to do them, but he was awkward. Whatever was asked of him, he attempted to do, but the others often did Salai's small jobs for themselves; it saved time in the end.

When Salai first came to the studio, Leonardo was working on various engineering jobs for Duke Ludovico Sforza, the ruler of Milan. Duke Ludovico was also called Il Moro, because his dark skin made him look like a Moor. Il Moro, a man proud of his inheritance as well as his accomplishments, had set Leonardo to working on a monument to his father. The monument was to be a statue of his father, seated upon a horse. Leonardo loved horses, and between his other duties for the duke he worked on designs for the giant statue. He often went to Il Moro's stables, where he sketched horses and studied them. He studied the similarities between their bones and their muscles and those of man. He had with him always paper and a piece of chalk or a pen. He sketched and took notes whenever he was thinking. And that was often.

Leonardo took Salai with him to the stables where he studied and sketched, his left hand moving across the page, creating pictures of his thoughts.

The first time Salai had seen Leonardo put his hand to paper, he had crossed himself. "What is the matter?" Leonardo had asked.

"Nothing," he had answered. But the boy had attempted to busy himself somewhere away from Leonardo. All the other young men in the workshop loved nothing more than to watch the master at work, and Salai, if he could, would leave the room.

One day as the two of them were alone at the stables, Leonardo was sketching the finest of Il Moro's Barbary horses and called Salai to him. Salai stood behind his master and stared at the ground. "Come here where I can see you, Salai," Leonardo said.

Salai moved to Leonardo's side, and Leonardo held him

in place with his right hand as he continued sketching with his left. "Duke Il Moro wants me to go to Pavia to consult with his architects about the dome for the cathedral."

"Yes, sir," Salai answered, keeping his eyes to the ground.

"Would you like to come with me to Pavia, Salai?"

"What part of town is that, sir?"

"Pavia is out of town. It is a day's journey from here."

Salai, who had never been out of Milan before, looked up, pleased. The corner of his eye caught the picture that Leonardo was causing to appear on the page, and he immediately lowered his eyes and crossed himself.

Leonardo smiled. "I asked you if you would like to come?"

Salai slowly raised his eyes, staring, fascinated by Leonardo's left hand, stroking the page. "Will we go on horseback, sir?"

"Yes."

"Are you now making the horse we'll take?"

"No," Leonardo said. "Il Moro does not allow his finest steeds to carry painters and their luggage."

"I mean the one on the page. Are you going to make it come alive after you've finished drawing it?"

"What makes you think I can do that?"

"Because you are drawing the horse with your left hand, sir," Salai answered.

"Yes," Leonardo replied, "my left hand has been given the greater talent."

"If God had given you your talent, you would be right-handed. God-power is right-handed. The left hand does the work of the Devil. I have often heard my father say, 'that horse has the Devil in him' or 'that horse bears the marks of the Devil.' "

Leonardo laughed. He looked straight at the boy and said, "I notice that you cut purses with your right hand. Are you doing God's work?"

"I cut no purse," Salai protested. "The thong was worn."

"Come, give me your hand, Salai," Leonardo said. Salai extended his left hand. Leonardo would not take it. "You are not left-handed, Salai. Now, come, give me your right hand."

Salai looked at his master and pleaded, "Please take my left hand, sir."

"Give me your right hand," Leonardo demanded.

Salai shut his eyes and produced his right hand. Leonardo laid it over the back of his left one. "Now look, Salai," he said. The boy's eyes were squeezed shut. "Look," Leonardo commanded. Salai opened his eyes. "I want you to feel the muscles and the movement of my hand. And I want you to notice that if I tell my hand to go left, it goes left." Leonardo swung his whole arm off the page. "And if I tell it to go right, it goes right." He swung his arm off the page on the opposite side. "It is I who guides that hand. My eye and my brain are joined to these muscles and tell them what to do." He paused and looked at the boy. "The Devil takes no part in my work." They moved their hands over the page, the young boy's fingertips riding the back of Leonardo's left hand, like lint on the wing of an eagle. Salai smiled; his hand was riding the back of creation. Leonardo stopped drawing, and Salai kept his hand on top of the master's.

"You may remove your hand now, Salai," he said. "Go pack our things. We leave for Pavia at dawn."

So Salai went off to pack, relieved, thinking, wondering why everyone was so in awe of master Leonardo da Vinci. He was not God; Salai had learned that the very first day, and now he just learned that he was not the Devil's helper, either. Leonardo was something in between God and the Devil. Well, so was he. So was he, Gian Giacomo de' Caprotti, called Salai.

Leonardo studied the buildings of Pavia; he walked through the streets in his long, flowing robe, quiet and contained, and sketched facts and ideas. He could not look at things made by God without wondering how He had made them, and he could not look at things made by man without thinking of some way to make them better. He thought of plans for a city that would keep the traffic of animals separated from the traffic of people. Such a city would keep his long cloak free from the sewage that seeped into the streets.

Leonardo met with other men, famous ones, who studied at the University of Pavia. They were expert mathematicians, architects and poets. All of them talked freely of the books they had read and the buildings they had seen and the plans they were making for the future. Leonardo did not talk very much at all. Salai noticed that the men would pause, look to Leonardo and wait for him to add his thoughts to theirs, but Leonardo never accepted their silent invitations.

One night as they walked to their quarters after a long discussion about whether Greek or Latin was the more noble language, Salai asked Leonardo which language he would have voted for if he had voted at all.

"If I were to cast a vote at all, it would be for Italian. Being the tongue of commerce, it has vigor."

"I'd vote Italian, too," Salai said, very positively. "It's hard enough reading words that sound like something you've heard. Imagine having to read words that don't sound like anything you've ever heard and then having to translate them into ones that you have. It just puts off making sense by two steps." Leonardo smiled at the boy's logic, and Salai, encouraged by that smile, continued. "I wish you would have said something to them, Leonardo. You should have voted Italian. Your vote would have counted a whole lot. You've read as many books as those guys."

Leonardo's smile faded. "No, Salai, I have not read as many books as they have. They are trained in the universities. I was a grown man before I learned Latin, and I had to teach myself. If I were to express an opinion to them, they could contradict it by citing Author A in Greek and Author B in Latin. It would not matter to them that my opinion was based upon observation. They believe nothing that they cannot read in a book."

The master's smile had altogether left him. Salai, who had learned to read people long before he had learned to read books, wanted that smile to return. He cleared his throat and said, "Reading books does make people very opinionated. As a matter of fact, it seems to me that to be very learned in books means only to have an opinion on other people's opinions." He looked up and read Leonardo's face and continued. "As soon as you finish teaching me how to read books, Master Leonardo, I'm going to make certain that I don't read too many."

"I don't think we're in any danger of that, Salai."

"I don't want to be like those guys. Why, they read books in three languages and have opinions in four." Salai noticed a grin beginning to play around his master's mouth. "Why, those guys," he continued, "would rather read about a horse than go look at one." The grin grew. "Why, those guys could get peed on by a horse, and they wouldn't know how they got wet if they couldn't look it up in a book. Why, those guys—"

Leonardo threw his head back and laughed, that strange, quiet laugh of his that pushed the sounds downward, a laughter as private as his thoughts. That laughter was what Salai had worked for. He never bothered to finish his sentence.

Until he had met Leonardo, Salai had never known anyone who lived by any principles other than superstition and survival. In his life on the streets survival had required that he be one thing in one situation and another in another. In his life in the studio he had quickly learned that superstition was out and that survival meant reading Leonardo's moods and supplying whatever color was needed. He could turn blush pink in one situation, be yellow in another and true blue in a third. His makeup was a whole palette. The color he carried in largest supply was laughter.

Salai could learn about the principles of art and learning, but he could not learn to care about them. He could pretend to care, as he pretended to care about the Latin or Greek issue. Yet it was not fair to say that Salai was insincere, for his very insincerity was sincere. And it was all stamped *self-preservation.* And with that instinct born of survival Salai knew that he was supplying Leonardo with something besides loyalty and shades of laughter, something that he could not define yet, but which he knew was seated somewhere in his attitude toward things that others —men of principle, men of wealth, men of learning—considered important.

THEY STAYED in Pavia until Duke Ludovico called them back to Milan. Leonardo took Salai with him to the castle, where they were guided to a large room. The duke was sitting in a tub of water, a tray of fruit stretched across the tub, and a lady sitting on a chair by the side of the tub, feeding him grapes one at a time. Salai started toward the tub, but Leonardo pulled him back.

"Is he naked under there?" Salai asked in a voice that for Salai passed as a whisper.

Leonardo did not answer; he only tugged at the boy's cloak, and Salai understood that he was to be quiet. Leonardo bowed before the tub, and Salai, glancing sideways at his master, did likewise, staying down until Leonardo patted him on his bottom as a signal that he should rise.

Ludovico lost no time in telling them what was on his mind. "My astrologers," he said, "have told me that January is a good time for me to get married."

"Congratulations, sir," Leonardo said. "Milan will rejoice to have its illustrious duke married at last. Those who love you are anxious that you produce an heir."

"My bride-to-be is of a noble and old house. Her sister is married to the Duke of Mantua, and her mother is a daughter of the King of Naples. They will, of course, attend the wedding. The wedding will be in Pavia, but the festival, Leonardo, will be held here in Milan. I need you to supervise the festivities. The festival will include a pageant, and we will have a parade."

"Yes, sir."

"You will be clever, Leonardo."

"Yes, sir."

"What will you do that will be clever, Leonardo?"

"I must think about it, sir. To plan quickly such an important event would not be wise."

"We don't have years, Leonardo. This is not a project like the monument of the horse. This must be brought to a finish by January."

"But, sir, that the horse is not finished is not altogether

23

my fault. I must remind you, my lord, that you have called upon me for many other jobs. I need only mention my work in Pavia to supervise the construction of the cathedral or my engineering work on your defenses outside the city or my designing machines for war, now . . ."

The duke raised a dark arm out of the water. "All right, Leonardo. I will tell you only this. For this festival I will spare no expense. I want a glorious pageant. Everything must be very impressive, Leonardo. I repeat: very."

"I will think of so grand a pageant, my lord, that your new wife will be convinced that she has married someone wealthier than the Pope."

"I'm not worried about convincing her of anything. Don't worry about her. She is young, only sixteen. She knows that I am rich; everyone knows where money is. There are others that need to be impressed. There are others who must see how cultured I am. I want them to experience my excellent taste. Everything must be rich and plentiful and original and clever and reflect my excellent and cultured mind. You must do glorious things, Leonardo. I command it."

"All shall be as you wish, my lord," Leonardo said.

As they turned to leave, the duke started to rise from the water. Salai hung back. Leonardo tugged at his sleeve, but the boy would not budge. The duke, being concerned with drying himself and applying scented oils, paid no attention.

"Hey, Leonardo," Salai called. Leonardo pretended that he did not hear and started walking toward the door, hoping that Salai would follow, but Salai did not. "Hey, Leonardo," Salai repeated. Leonardo continued walking, not turning around. "Leonardo, look!" Salai shouted, pointing. "He's as dark as a Moor all over." Leonardo, his face frozen, swung back around into the room and grabbed Salai by his collar and pulled him from the room. Salai kept stealing looks up at his master, knowing that he had done something wrong, but not knowing what. Leonardo walked rapidly out of the room and was halfway across the courtyard before he stopped.

He then threw his head back and laughed, a genuine, peasant-style guffaw. "Dark as a Moor all over," he said, and then broke into laughter again. "Dark as a Moor all over," he repeated.

"Salai," he said, "I think that where the Lord gave most men a bump for respect, He gave you a hollow."

LEONARDO gave himself up entirely to plans for the festival. He quit making sketches of horses; he quit studying rivers and mountains; he quit studying mathematics and anatomy. He became for the time of the preparations a combination of magician and housewife.

He invented a stage which revolved. (Magician.) When the workmen used up their supply of paint and attempted to finish the job with a new batch which did very nearly but did not quite match, he made them start all over again. (Housewife.) He designed costumes for the tournaments; one set of men were to look like Moors and another to look like Scythians. (Magician.) When in the rush of things the tailors took stitches that were too long, Leonardo ripped out the whole seam. (Housewife.)

Salai was sent scurrying here and there, gathering materials and delivering Leonardo's instructions. He visited his father and his sister and reported to them that the chefs were designing cakes and pastries in the shapes of unicorns and dragons. "So you see," he said to Dorotea, "in a castle you even *eat* works of art." Dorotea crossed herself when Salai told her that.

The boy enjoyed his duties. He never had the feeling that others had—that they were being kept from something important to do the unimportant, menial jobs around the studio. Salai had a well-developed sense of unimportance. And now with the festival everything seemed less serious than usual, and *less serious* suited Salai as much as *less important* did.

Strangely enough, Leonardo, who was very serious, serious about himself, serious about his work, enjoyed the preparations for the festivities, too.

"Festival," he explained to Salai, "is like lightning. It has no history, and it has no future. It lights up everything for a brief second. It passes. It leaves nothing of itself save its effect. The lightning itself is never there to be pawed over by future generations. A pageant, dear Salai, gives an artist a chance to zigzag through time like lightning, like a wild, irresponsible thing."

Salai listened to Leonardo, grateful to have him lighthearted. Leonardo was usually so concerned with the future that he couldn't relax in the now. Salai realized that a genius person like Leonardo should be concerned with the future, and he was glad that he was not a genius. Merely being quick and smart was perfectly all right with him. His life had always been a conglomeration of *nows*. He had never postponed a small happiness for the sake of a future larger one. Salai's whole life had been a festival, a wild streak, an irresponsible zigzag in Renaissance time.

"I hope," Salai said, "that the duke's wife has more than one head and more than one set of eyes in each of those heads. Otherwise, she will not be able to see everything that you have planned for her."

"These elaborations are not for her, Salai," Leonardo answered. "Remember, the duke said that he is not worried about convincing her of anything. All this effort is for Isabella and for Cecilia."

Salai, who loved good gossip second to anise cookies, asked Leonardo to explain. And Leonardo, who also loved good gossip but pretended he did not, did. As they worked, he told Salai the story of how, after a ten-year engagement, the Duke of Milan came at last to set his wedding date.

Ten years ago Il Moro had wanted to marry Beatrice's sister, Isabella d'Este. Isabella was eight years old at the time, and Il Moro was twenty-nine, but word had spread throughout Italy about how beautiful and gifted was this first child of the Duke and Duchess of Ferrara. Il Moro decided to claim her and wait. He was in no hurry to marry. He had enemies and dukedoms to conquer while Isabella finished growing up. It was an altogether suitable match, so Ludovico rode to Ferrara and offered himself as a suitor. He arrived exactly two weeks too late. The Duke of Ferrara had just promised Isabella to Gonzaga, the son of the Duke of Mantua.

Isabella's father did not want the possibility of a connection to the wealth of Milan to pass him by. He knew that he could not withdraw his promise to Gonzaga, so he made a counterproposal to Il Moro. Why not, he asked, marry Beatrice, his second daughter, instead? She was but two years younger than Isabella; she was not as pretty nor as vivacious, but she carried the same noble blood in her veins; and he would guarantee that her dowry would be as large as her sister's.

Just as the Duke of Ferrara did not want to offend the Duke of Mantua, the Duke of Milan did not want to offend the Duke of Ferrara; war was always just an insult away. So Il Moro agreed to marry Beatrice. The Duke of Ferrara hoped that eight years from that day his two daughters would be married in a double ceremony.

But that had not happened. Isabella had married Gonzaga a year ago, but Ludovico still had not claimed Beatrice. He found first one excuse and then another. Affairs of state, he claimed. But Beatrice's father was no fool; he knew that the wedding had been postponed not for affairs of state but for an affair of the heart. Rumors of Il Moro's love for Cecília Gallerani had reached Ferrara, and the father of the bride-to-be hinted that he was equally prepared for a wedding or for a war. Il Moro suddenly consulted his astrologers and set a wedding date.

There had never been any doubt in Milan that Cecilia Gallerani was Ludovico's great love. In the nine years that Leonardo had been in Il Moro's city, the only time that the duke had requested a portrait was the time he had asked the master to paint Cecilia. Leonardo had painted her holding an ermine in her arms, and he had succeeded in showing the bright, the self-assured, the amused look of the lady as reflected by the bright look of the ermine. Leonardo had painted her hands with great care, for what the face did not show of the lady's character, those long, expressive, competent fingers did.

"These exertions for the wedding festival are more for Cecilia and Isabella than they are for Beatrice. The duke wants the ladies to see what they have missed," Leonardo concluded.

As Salai listened to Leonardo, he busied himself grinding pigments. He noticed the other apprentices eyeing him. He knew that being a favorite of Leonardo exposed him to envy among his fellows. The others were jealous of anyone who received an extra dollop of Leonardo's attention. Thank goodness, he thought, that he was not talented, too. Salai gladly shared any information he received from the master, for neither jealousy nor a sense of privacy was well developed in him. But the apprentices wanted to learn from Leonardo himself. They suffered from an ailment common to the times: they took themselves seriously. Very seriously.

Leonardo never spent a lot of time trying to develop their talents. When one of them ran into difficulty with some work, Leonardo usually picked up the appropriate tool—brush or knife or crayon—and quietly corrected the work, mumbling "like so" as he worked. Sometimes Leonardo would get so involved with the work he was correcting that he would stand at the easel a whole morning, brushing life into it, mumbling "like so" as the student watched and tried to make reasons and rules for Leonardo's instincts. When pressed, Leonardo would tell them that he was writing a book on painting and that they would find all his reasons there. Leonardo demanded that his students be neat. They often complained to each other that to be Leonardo's apprentice meant learning to keep one's blues in a row separated from one's greens and learning to interpret one mumbled "like so" from another.

Outside of the studio, they never uttered a single complaint. In the court of Milan to be a pupil of Leonardo da

Vinci was to be touched with grace, like being cardinal to the Pope in Rome. Those whose ambitions outran their talents liked it that way. Leonardo did, too.

None of his pupils was greatly gifted. Salai least of all.

Leonardo whose father had never married his mother, Leonardo who had gone late as an apprentice to Verrocchio, Leonardo who had no fortune of his own, Leonardo who had to count on the gifts of his hand and his head— this Leonardo never felt certain that he had a place. This Leonardo never felt comfortable in the presence of dukes or of university men. This Leonardo was not willing to allow his seeds to fall on fertile ground where they might grow, for this Leonardo was not willing to cultivate his own replacement.

Leonardo kept his thoughts and his opinions to himself and to his notebooks. What he allowed to spill over, spilled over to Salai, that small desert of talent. Leonardo's waters could nourish nothing there; there was no talent to cultivate, and no one to turn a hoe. Salai was clever, but he was not creative. He would never blossom into a great artist. Leonardo and Salai both knew that, and they both accepted it. Salai was the chosen because he was sensitive —which made him a good audience—and not serious— which made him no threat.

T HE VERY RICH and the very titled did not come to the studio. Leonardo went to them.

One evening while frantically finishing preparations for the tournaments, Leonardo and Salai went to the house of San Severino. They carried with them the costumes of the Scythians. When they arrived, the footmen who were to take part in the tournament took off the clothes they were wearing and tossed them onto a couch and began to rummage around the assortment of garments, pulling out a pair of trousers and a jerkin that would fit. They tried on one thing and another and took time out to admire themselves and each other with each garment they added.

"Ah, Master Leonardo, you are a genius."

"Whatever Leonardo touches turns into a work of art."

"Ah, Leonardo, you are much too smart for one man."

Salai stood aside and listened. This was not praise; this was talk. Talk, talk, talk. Taste with no mind of its own. These were words thrown at Leonardo as one throws seeds to the pigeons of the piazza.

One gentleman named Francesco called to Leonardo. "I must see you a minute." He pulled the master aside and engaged him in private conversation for a full five minutes. Leonardo nodded several times and smiled several others, but he said as little as he ever did. Francesco walked away from Leonardo and rejoined the group, "Oh," he announced, "Leonardo quite agrees with me. . . ."

Salai sat there on the couch on top of the heap of jackets and listened to them. They were not worth Leonardo's attention. But there he was, repeating the same answers to the same compliments. There he was accepting praise from this unrefined, uneducated bunch of men, no more grown up—except for height—than Salai himself. They were deaf men praising a concert. No. They were worse, for they could hear, but they would not. They were overgrown puppies standing between a saucer of meat and a mother's teat: knowing that the saucer is full of nourishment but too lazy to chew, content to be told what is in the saucer as they continue suckling and telling each other how close they came to tasting solid food.

So this was Leonardo's audience. A flock of grackles: noisy, wearing glossy plumage, mindless. Leonardo deserved better; he deserved *informed* appreciators.

Salai rested on top of that heap of jackets and rolled over to face the wall, to face away from them. As he turned, he heard the jingle of coins. His hands began to explore first one jacket and then another, and when he found the coins he pocketed them as quietly as he had explored for them. He stayed on the couch as long as he could. He stayed there until Leonardo called for him to help the men undress.

It was Francesco who missed his money. Before he said anything he went over to the couch and searched in, around and under it. Then he hurried over to his host, San Severino, and whispered something to him. San Severino smiled and nodded. "It seems," he announced to the group, "that Francesco has lost some money. Perhaps someone picked it up by mistake. Let's do this," he said. He pulled a small table into the middle of the room. "Let us all turn our backs to the table, face the wall and close our eyes. Then the person who accidentally picked up Francesco's purse can return it, and he won't be embarrassed. San Severino looked right at Salai as he said that. Salai returned his look, no blush, no blink. They started to turn to face the wall, and San Severino said, "I'll count to thirty, and then we'll all turn back."

Everyone, even Francesco, began to regard catching the

thief as a game. There was laughter as they all turned around to face the wall. San Severino counted slowly, and when he reached *thirty* everyone turned around expectantly, but the table was bare. Disappointed, but determined to remain cheerful, San Severino said, "All right, all right, that was just a trial. Now I want everyone to quietly search for the missing money. This time we will turn around after the count of thirty-five." They all turned to face the wall again.

While they were turned, they heard someone walk up to the table very quietly. There were two thieves present, Salai thought. Then he got mad; someone else got part of Francesco's money. This time everyone fidgeted until San Severino finished his counting.

Thirty-one. Thirty-two. Thirty-three. Thirty-four
Thirty-five.

Everyone swung around and saw a piece of paper in the middle of the table. San Severino swaggered over and, smiling, picked it up. Everyone looked at the spot under the paper. Empty. San Severino looked at the paper, turned it over and grabbed the seat of his pants. Francesco reached for the paper and read it: "Don't turn your back on us again, Severino. Your pants are ripped."

The theft and the game dissolved into laughter, and Francesco did not recover his wallet. Salai felt relieved to know that there was not another thief in the place.

As they walked home, Leonardo said, "You took Francesco's wallet, did you not, Salai?"

"I, sir? No, sir."

"Confess now. I will not reveal you to the crowd. I shall quietly return it. By messenger. They will never know. I would simply like the truth from you. Confess, Salai."

"I did not take it, Master Leonardo."

"I think you did, Salai."

"Far be it from me, sir, to argue with what the greatest mind in all of Milan thinks."

"Don't offer hollow compliments, Salai. When you sound like San Severino's friends, you earn only my contempt. Did you take the wallet, Salai."

"No, Master."

"Well, perhaps Francesco deserves to be a little embarrassed."

"Yes, sir," the boy said.

SALAI waited until the day that Duchess Beatrice was to enter the city of Milan to spend his ill-gotten money. The streets were jammed. It was like a carnival, but better, because nothing was worn out or being used for even the second time. Leonardo had had new clothes made for him: a gold brocade vest and parti-colored hose. He stood before his master, and Leonardo reached for a comb and rearranged his curls. There was no detail involving beauty that was too small to command Leonardo's attention. He lay the comb down, studied the effect, his head tilted, then he took a few stray curls in between his fingers and placed them behind the boy's ears. He turned the young man around and pointed him toward the door. "Go, Salai. See it all."

The boy wandered alone through the streets. He found a vendor of sweets on the street of the armorers and bought from him his entire supply of anise comfits. He silently thanked Francesco when he noted that he still had some coins left.

Salai, dressed in his very best, surveyed Milan, dressed in its very best. Walls and balconies were hung with satin in bright colors and brocades woven with threads of gold. Chains of ivy were draped over doorways and wrapped around columns. But the best street of all was the one where Salai walked, the street of the armor-makers.

Both sides of the avenue were lined with straw men on wooden horses. They were dressed in chain mail and plates of steel. The straw men carried lances, and Salai was more pleased than if they had been alive. For now they stayed still and Salai could entertain himself by examining the engraved pictures on the steel breast plates. He thought that if they were laid end to end they would tell the story of every battle of every war. Even the wars of the gods of ancient Rome. Salai considered it far better to learn history from such scenes than from reading. Reading took a lot more effort.

He ambled along the street of the armorers, eating his sweets, trying to limit himself to one cake per stop, but some of the men in armor were so interesting that he stopped for a long time, and he allowed himself two, sometimes three. From the street of the armorers he walked to the piazza in front of the castle. There the crowd was thick. He could easily have worked his way to the front of the crowd, using the techniques he had learned in his days of picking pockets. But the smell of the crowd held him back like a harness. Only months before he would never have noticed that the people had an odor at all, but living with Leonardo, he had grown accustomed to sweet smells. For his visits home he had begun to carry a perfumed handkerchief to sniff.

He reached in his sack for more cookies and found that they were all gone. He felt relieved that they were. Had there been more, he didn't know if he could bear the responsibility of finishing them. He tried to penetrate the crowd again when he heard a hundred trumpets. The crowd called, "She comes! She comes!" Everyone pressed closer toward the edge of the piazza, and Salai felt the weight and smell of the mob create a force that propelled him from the center. He gave up hope of seeing the duchess arrive.

Then Francesco, the absent Francesco, came to his rescue. Salai reached in his pocket and took a coin from it. He poked the tallest man within range of his arm. "I'll give you this if you let me stand on your shoulders," Salai said. The man took the coin and boosted Salai up.

Ludovico and his bride stopped at the entrance to the castle. All the nobles were waiting there for them. The duchess was lifted down from her carriage, and as she was, a hush seemed to pass through the crowd.

Salai looked at the new duchess from his perch upon the man's shoulders. "Why, she's small and dark and perfectly plain," he said. And after pronouncing judgment, he drew in a deep breath and was overwhelmed by nausea.

His throat slid upward, and he spilled his cookies all over the man in front of him as well as the top of the man whose shoulders he had rented.

THE WEDDING festivities went on for a week. Leonardo was called upon to do everything. He even designed the shelves for the display of the wedding gifts. These small jobs kept him from his important work, and Leonardo both loved and hated that.

Toward the end of the week, the festivities included a play for which Leonardo had designed the costumes and a revolving stage. The play was called *Paradise*, and it was a great success. After the performance Salai had gone to bed late and with his head pounding from having emptied the unfinished wine glasses. He awoke to a great pounding at the door and a voice proclaiming, "Prepare yourselves. Prepare yourselves."

Salai pulled the covers over his ears. He couldn't distinguish between the pounding in his head and the pounding on the door. *Prepare yourselves* could only mean that he had died (it had been a bad, bad night) and that the forces of the Devil had won the toss-up for his soul. How unfair, he thought, to be but a boy and to have the appetites of a man.

"Answer the door, Salai," Leonardo called.

"Door? Door, master?"

"Someone wants our attention."

"Oh, yes, master," Salai said. He jumped out of bed into the cold room, the quickest he had ever done so. He usually poked out one toe, then one foot and allowed each knuckle to adjust to the air outside his blankets. But this morning, Salai thought, the colder the better; the colder, the farther he was from the fires of Hell.

"Prepare yourself," the door-pounder yelled again.

It was only a fifty-second walk from his bed to the door, but that was all the time it took for Salai to change from gratitude at not being called to the Gates of Hell to annoyance at being called to the gates of the studio.

And when he looked through the window and saw that it was a page no older than himself who had ordered him to prepare himself, his annoyance became total. He opened the door just as the young man once again called, "Prepare yourself."

"For what?" answered Salai.

"Prepare yourself for a visit from the Duchess Leonora and her daughter, the Duchess Isabella."

The two boys looked each other over. Salai was bothered that such a fellow should catch him in his nightshirt. His new suit, the one that Leonardo had had made for the festival, was not as fancy as the page's but nicer.

"Who are Leonora and Isabella?" Salai asked.

"The Duchess Isabella is the sister to the Duchess Beatrice, and the Duchess Leonora is the mother to the Duchess Isabella as well as the Duchess Beatrice. That same Duchess Beatrice who is the wife of the Duke Ludovico Sforza, called Il Moro." He lowered his nose and asked, "Did you not know that?"

"Who might this Il Moro be?" Salai asked.

The page gasped. "Is this not the home and workshop of Leonardo da Vinci? Even the stray cats of Milan know who is Il Moro, I mean Duke Il Moro."

"The name sounds a little familiar," Salai said. "But the other. Leonardo da Vinci . . . does every stray cat in Milan know that name too?"

"Even I know. I am from Mantua."

"Mantua?" Salai asked, "Is that the street next to the sewer?"

44

The page gasped, "Why, Mantua is the home of Isa-bella, I mean the Duchess Isabella, the sister of Beatrice, I mean Duchess Beatrice—"

At that moment Leonardo came to the door. "Enough, Salai. Go get dressed." Leonardo ran his hand over the top of Salai's head. He then turned to the page and said, "Tell the Duchesses Leonora and Isabella that their servant Leo-nardo da Vinci awaits their visit. With pleasure."

"How do *you* know?" the page asked.

"I am a stray cat," Leonardo answered. "Now, go. Tell them I am ready."

The minute the door was closed, Salai told Leonardo what he thought of stuck-up, self-important pages. "Those guys, boss, are like a collection of jewelry, only not as val-uable. Did you see how fancy—I'd like to see one of them, just one, have to be an artist's apprentice once, just once. I'd like to see one of them having to cook up glue and var-nish. I'd like to see what would happen to their fancy clothes after they put in a full day's work."

"They do put in a full day's work, Salai."

"Yeah, sure. Just putting on all those clothes is a full day's work."

"They clean stables, Salai."

The boy stopped short. "You mean they pitch horse manure dressed liked that?"

"No, Salai, dressed like that they tell artists and apprentices to prepare themselves. Now, suppose you do that. Suppose you get dressed. The ladies will be here shortly. When they arrive, Salai, I would like you to be beautiful and mute."

Both duchesses were beautiful. Isabella was a younger, thinner, more delicate version of her mother. Next to the two of them, Il Moro's new wife looked like the print of the page for which they were the colored illustrations. Poor, plain Beatrice. No wonder that Il Moro, a man greatly interested in appearances, had made Isabella his first choice.

Salai focused his attention on Isabella. She wore a semismile. It was not a happy smile, though; her eyes were not a part of it. Salai had seen a smile like that before. Francesco. Francesco, looking in the mirror as he had tried on his costume for the festival. Yes, Beatrice's sister was one of those. She wore the smile of one who lived in a private bubble of good thoughts about herself.

The Duchess Isabella lost no time at all in letting Leonardo know the purpose of her visit. She would like some painting done by Leonardo. "I already have an admirable collection; your work will reside in good company. The first work I would like from you is a portrait of myself. I would like a portrait done with the same delicate shading you used in the portrait of Cecilia Gallerani, but I would not like to pose with a weasel. Next I should like a portrait

46

of a young Christ. First me and then Jesus. I shall arrange with my sister and brother-in-law for the loan of you. I cannot imagine Il Moro refusing my request. I shall pose from 10:00 until 12:00 on Mondays and Thursdays."

Leonardo knew that he was an employee; he also knew that he was fortunate in having as an employer a man who gave him as much freedom as Il Moro did. He would not mind working for Duchess Isabella as a favor to Il Moro; he certainly owed his patron that much. But the thought of being *loaned* as they loaned each other dwarfs and jesters, that thought was despicable. And the thought of having to paint Isabella every Monday and every Thursday —to know that his work would be held together by two such bars of time—was to make a prison of his week. Leonardo was well schooled in the manners of the court. "My dearest lady," he said, "I would be most delighted to do your portrait. I am certain that the Duke Il Moro will not mind my postponing my work on the model of the horse for the monument to his illustrious father. My work on the monument has been delayed many times. I am certain that the duke will not mind a longer delay. When he asks, tell him I estimate only a year and a half to complete your assignments in Mantua."

Isabella lifted an eyebrow. "I understand," she said. "Never let it be said that anyone understands talent better than I. If it is not possible for you to come to Mantua, I

47

would like then some small piece of sculpture. Something you can work on in your studio here. You should be very flattered, Leonardo, that I want something from your hand. I am very selective about the works I accumulate. I think that a small bust of the young Christ would be a very nice thing to own."

Salai knew that Leonardo did not like sculpture. The work was messy. Sculptors, he had written in his notebooks, create their work by the strength of their arms, and this is accomplished only by great sweat which mixes with the marble dust. The marble dust spreads over everything like flour, so that you cannot tell if you have in your studio a baker or an artist. A painter, on the other hand, sits before his work in a clean house, at ease, well-dressed, and listens to music as he dips his brush in delicate color. So Isabella wanted either her portrait done or a work of sculpture? Was there nothing she could propose that would have appeal? It took every ounce of Salai's will to keep quiet.

Leonardo tried to say something, but he was not quick enough, for no sooner had Isabella proposed a small piece of sculpture, a small bust of the young Christ, than she looked around the room and lowered her eyes just enough for them to fall on Salai. "This child will do," she said. "Come here, boy. What is your name? Never mind. I don't want to know. If he is to be a model for Christ, it is better that he have no name. Giving him a name can only give him personal prestige. It detracts from the work, don't you think? You see, Leonardo, I am not unversed in the arts. I do have ideas. You must come to Mantua some time so that we can discuss theories of art. It will be a real exchange of ideas." She got up. "Come along, Mother," she said. She paused at the door and added, "Send me sketches. My dear sister Beatrice and my beloved brother-in-law have promised to write every day. Every single day. You may use their messengers. I'll speak to Beatrice about it. No. On second thought, I'll speak to Il Moro. He can't refuse me anything, it seems."

She and her mother nodded goodbye, and they left.

Leonardo leaned back against the closed door and shook his head as if he had just come up from under water. He held his hands over his ears.

"Well, boss," Salai said, "there is no need ever again to tell me to be mute in the presence of Duchess Isabella. My only wish is that in her presence I were also deaf." Salai paused and added, "Are you going to pose me for the young Christ?"

"I shall start on it after all of my other duties are finished."

"By then I shall have as great a beard as yours," Salai said.

Leonardo smiled, and so did Salai.

FROM THE TIME of the wedding festivities until the middle of March, Il Moro shipped his young wife first to one castle and then to another. She traveled with ample company; San Severino, Francesco and their friends and her many ladies-in-waiting accompanied her. They fished and hunted during the day and played scartino and backgammon in the evenings. While Beatrice moved from home to home, Il Moro chose to stay in Milan to look after his affairs of state (and Cecilia Gallerani).

During this time Leonardo was engaged in a study of mountains and rivers. He walked great distances in order to sketch the entire view from the mountain or a single wind-blown tree. High in the mountains he had discovered seashells that had turned to stone, and he wanted to know how they had gotten there. He wondered long and wandered far to discover the reason that seashells were on a mountaintop; and he often forgot to eat. Salai had gotten into the habit of taking him food.

Salai had packed some cheese and bread, a small bottle of wine and some fresh anise cakes for his master. There was one anise cake for Leonardo and six altogether.

On his way to the mountain to find his master, Salai walked across the inner court of the castle, his sack slung over his shoulder. He was halfway across the courtyard when he heard someone call from the far corner, "I'm over here."

Salai stopped and saw the Duchess Beatrice sitting in the sun, her hair pulled through the open crown of a wide-brimmed hat. 'I'm over here," she repeated, "trying to get the sun to make me blond and beautiful."

Salai walked over. The young duchess looked him over —up and down—and announced, "You're very well proportioned for a dwarf."

"Yes, my lady," Salai replied.

"That's all right," she said, "I have no objections to a well-proportioned dwarf. Let me see what you can do."

"Do?" he asked.

"Yes. *Do*," she repeated. "My sister, Isabella, says that you can juggle and do acrobatics and that when you are very jolly, you do your imitation of a drunken monk, and that is certain to cheer me up."

"Oh, yes," Salai answered. If someone needed cheering up, how could he not try? He had seen enough drunk monks, but he didn't think he could start with that. "I shall juggle first," he said.

"What will you juggle?"

He reached into his sack and pulled out an anise cookie. "This!" he exclaimed, and he then began tossing it from one hand to another. "Loop de loo. Loop de la," he cooed.

"Is that it?" Beatrice asked. "When will you toss two at a time?"

"Right now!" Salai answered. He reached into the sack again and withdrew another anise cookie. "Are you sure you are ready for this?" he asked. The young duchess nodded. Salai looked at the cookies, knowing that the minute he tried to keep two in the air, one, at least, would go splat. Oh, well, he thought, Leonardo's will be the first to go.

One anise cake did go splat immediately. He looked down at it, and could not bear to leave it there for the ants. The second that he looked down, the other went splat also. Salai followed that second cookie to the ground, and began to pick up pieces and to eat them right there.

The duchess got up from her chair and sniffed the

cookies. "Anise?" she asked. Salai nodded, not raising his eyes, picking up crumbs to stuff into his mouth. The duchess began to do the same. "I love anise," she said. "But don't let me eat too much. I have vowed not to get fat. Mother is fat, and Isabella will get there, but not I."

"Isabella will keep a lean tongue," Salai said. "She overworks it."

Duchess Beatrice laughed, her whole mouth open, her tongue and teeth coated with wet anise cookie, the uninhibited laugh of someone who would never let good manners interfere with a need as strong as laughter. "Have you another anise cake?" she asked. "An uncrushed one?" Salai nodded. "I know what!" she said. "You do a trick to make it appear. Make it just appear. You are very good at doing magic, Isabella says."

"In Mantua *Isabella says* is one word. We call her *Isabellasays*. In Mantua we do not allow the fair Duchess Isabellasays in the sun without an umbrella; we fear that she will get a sunburned tongue."

"Oh, Matello!" Beatrice exclaimed.

At that moment Salai saw a dwarf coming from the far end of the court. Apparently, the real Matello had come forward. Beatrice, who was not facing the direction from which he was coming, could not see him. "Close your eyes, Duchess," Salai said. "Close your eyes, and I shall have for you a surprise bigger than an anise cookie." Beatrice obliged, and Salai motioned to the dwarf to hurry over. Matello toddled over, his large head weaving, his shoulders lifting and falling with each step. Salai held his finger over his mouth, and the dwarf obligingly kept quiet. Salai set one anise cake in each of the dwarf's hands and popped one into his mouth. "Open your eyes, my lady," he called.

Beatrice looked from Matello to Salai and back again. And then, as daintily as you please, she plucked one, then two, then three cookies from the little man. She examined the one from his mouth, made a small face and popped it back between his thick lips. "That one is yours for keeps." She took one of the other two and held it within Salai's reach. Just as Salai raised his hand to take it, she swung it behind her back. "It will be yours," she said, "when you tell me who you are."

"I am Salai," he said.

"And I am Beatrice d'Este, wife of Ludovico Sforza, Il Moro as he is called, the Duke of Milan."

"I know who you are," Salai replied. "I've seen you before. I threw up the first time I saw you."

"Well," Beatrice said, "I am certainly not as beautiful as you, but I had no idea that plain looks could upset your stomach."

"It was probably the anise cookies I ate that day."

At that she popped the cake she was holding out to him behind her back again. "What do you do besides throw up?" she asked.

"Why," he answered, "I am assistant to Leonardo da Vinci. Just now I was on my way to the mountains. He wants my advice on some scientific problems that have been puzzling him. Did you like the revolving stage that I invented for the production of *Paradise*?"

"Yes, I liked that very much, Salai. Tell me, how many men were required to turn it?"

"Not too many," Salai answered. "Only about four or eight thousand."

"Tell me, Salai, did you design the men, too? For you made them very quiet. I could have sworn that your four or eight thousand men moving the stage made no more sound than half a dozen of the usual type."

"Oh, yes," Salai replied, "I am very good at man-design. I specialize in designing quiet ones. I have one model that makes no sounds at all. Now listen and tell me if you can hear me." With that Salai moved his mouth, forming the words *Duchess Beatrice is a beautiful lady*, letting no sound escape his lips.

Beatrice watched Salai's lips very closely, she nodded her head and then clicked her tongue. "That was not a success, Salai. I heard it. I heard *Salai is the biggest liar in all of Milan*."

At that moment Salai looked into the eyes of the duchess, and she looked into his eyes, too. They exchanged a look that bound them together for that moment and for years to come. Because each found in the eye of the other

55

something he could appreciate. Both could recognize a genuine sense of mischief. Their look held until the smiles that were creeping up on their faces forced their eyes out of focus. Then they laughed, the soft laugh that comes when one sees a baby take its first steps, a laugh of rediscovery.

Beatrice said, "Now, Salai, I want you to observe how very excellent I am at silent sounds." She then moved her lips in a pattern that was easy to read, *"Tell Matello to go home."* Then out loud she added, "Would you do that for me please, Salai?"

"Certainly, my lady." Salai turned to Matello and said, "The Duchess Beatrice no longer needs you. She would like you to return to your mistress, the Duchess Isabella-says, and tell her that her sister, Beatrice, misses her very much, as much as a person with chicken pox misses the measles."

The dwarf looked from Salai to Beatrice and back again and again. Beatrice said, "You translated that very well, Salai." She smiled at the dwarf, took pity on his confusion and said, "You may go, Matello. I am quite cheered up."

As the little man went skipping back into the castle, Beatrice asked Salai, "Where are you going now?"

"To the mountains."

"Oh, yes," she said, "to consult with Leonardo about some scientific problems on the mountaintop." She bolted upright in the chair. "I'm going with you," she proclaimed. "Have you enough lunch in that sack for me, too?"

"Enough of everything except anise cookies."

THEY FOUND Leonardo sitting on the ground, turning over in his hand a wild flower he had picked. Salai had seen him study weeds for hours at a time. Once he had asked, "What are you doing, Master Leonardo?" and Leonardo had answered, "Watching grass." Salai had grown accustomed to long silences and strange answers.

The young duchess walked over to where Leonardo sat twirling the plant between his fingers. She reached over his shoulder from behind and took it from him. "The star of Bethlehem," she said.

Leonardo looked up, startled. He started to rise. Beatrice

put a hand on his shoulder with just enough pressure to tell him to remain seated. "Master Leonardo," she said, "were you to draw this humble weed, you would grant it immortality."

"You are very kind, my lady," Leonardo replied, turning to look at her.

Beatrice returned his look, long and steady. "No," she said. "I am not very kind. I am just kind. What I am very is: honest. I am very honest. And I am also very neglected."

"But, my lady, how can the wife to the richest duke in all of Italy feel neglected? Are you not surrounded by admirers and people willing to do your service?"

"I am, Master Leonardo. And so are you. But how does it conquer loneliness to have admirers who know what I am but do not know who I am? How does it conquer loneliness to have not one single person who sees something other than a plain brown wrapping and the label *Duchess* written thereon? Had my coloring been blond and had my features been elegant, as are my sister's, then people would care to look inside. They would find, Leonardo, bright colors inside this puce package. They would find an eye for every shade of every color of the rainbow and an ear for every quarter tone of the lute. They would find blood that pulses to every tincture and every texture and every taste." The duchess paused. "Except anise," she said, smiling toward Salai. "My taste for anise has been temporarily dulled."

Leonardo studied the young duchess. "You are plain, my lady," he pronounced. He looked at the star of Bethlehem which he held in his hand. "What an inconspicuous flower comes from this whorl of leaves. It was the whorl of leaves that I was studying. Can you make your leaf structure more interesting than that inconspicuous flower of your face?"

"It already is, Master Leonardo. But everyone is not Leonardo da Vinci. Everyone is not interested in looking at an inconspicuous flower. My husband is thirty-nine years old. He is a worldly man, and he is in love with one of the most beautiful and most intelligent women in Milan. He rushed back to her, to Milan, from our wedding in Pavia. I know why I am now being shipped about, but I say nothing to him. I am as tongue-tied with him as I was with my mother and sister. At home I was my parents' second daughter, my mother's second thought, and here I am second choice. Could I but gain my husband's love, I know that I could disguise this plain brown wrapping."

"Don't disguise it," Leonardo said. "Make it transparent. Sit down, my lady," Leonardo said. Beatrice sat, Leonardo spoke to her very quietly, very confidentially. "Your husband is a busy man. He is an impatient man also. But—for all his desire to show off, for all his need to surround himself with beautiful things and beautiful people—he has something that makes him the best patron in all of Italy. Better than the Medici of Florence. He can recognize the genuine from the sham, the original from the copy. He may not know why something is good, but he knows that it is, and he is willing to give that which is good his support. He has an instinct for true quality. He can detect quality in a horse, in a man, in a painting, and in a woman. He can appreciate it, delight in it. But dear lady, you are right; he will not take the time to look for it. He respects talent, but it must be brought to his attention. What original quality do you have to give him that Cecilia has not?"

"A sense of fun, Master Leonardo."

"Then give him that, dear lady. That will lead him toward your soul. A sense of fun is sadly lacking in our times."

"Hey, Duchess," Salai said, "I didn't know that you knew about Cecilia."

"Salai, had I your regular features and your golden curls, people would worry about what I think. People don't like to upset a beautiful thing. Were I as beautiful as Cecilia, I, too, would like to have my portrait painted by Leonardo da Vinci."

"You ought to let Leonardo paint you. He is the guy who believes that you paint a face to show what is inside the head. Besides," Salai continued, "Leonardo now has me to help him."

The little duchess lowered her eyes and said, half to

herself, "Perhaps. Perhaps, yes. But I think no. Perhaps there is too much vanity within me. Or perhaps I have too much respect for the master's talent. Would it be fair to have him who can create light on canvas be saddled with painting a face that should remain in shadow?"

"Listen," Salai said, "Leonardo draws all kind of funny faces. He draws grotesques all the time. There are pages of them all over the studio."

"My face is something between grotesque and beautiful, Salai. It is something far less interesting; it is plain."

"I like it," Salai said.

"And so do I," Leonardo added.

The young duchess sighed, then smiled. "Let's eat," she said.

AFTER THAT DAY in the mountains Beatrice often sent for Salai. Leonardo would excuse the boy from his duties in the shop, and Salai would attend to the duchess. Leonardo often joined them in the evenings.

Because Leonardo visited Beatrice, others soon followed. They came because of the master; they stayed because of the duchess. Evenings in her chambers were filled with poetry being read and songs being sung and music being played. All of that was in the air plus one other ingredient that Salai knew was magic.

Salai was convinced that Beatrice was a magician. He

noticed that four people in a room could sit in each other's presence and stifle yawns but that the same four people plus Beatrice suddenly had a great deal to say to each other. Even the secretive, self-conscious Leonardo began to fill the pages of his notebooks with stories and fables to read to her; he began to invent riddles, very complicated and intellectual and too difficult for everyone to understand. But everyone enjoyed seeing the master relax enough to tell them.

Evenings with Beatrice were spent indoors in the pursuit of art, but afternoons with her were spent out-of-doors in the pursuit of pure pleasure. Francesco and his grackles were good company in the afternoon. They all enjoyed fishing and riding and hunting and just plain fooling around. Beatrice often made up elaborate games and jokes; nothing suited Salai more.

Beatrice once asked Salai to bring her one of his sister's most miserable dresses. She gave Dorotea one of her good brocade gowns in exchange. With both she and Salai dressed in old, faded clothing, she then gave him a dirty sack and filled it with gold ducats. Before he could sling it over his shoulder, she laid on top of the pile of money ten large dried, salted flounder. Then they invaded the shop of the silversmith. When he saw them arrive, the merchant tried to shoo them away before any of his customers could see them or smell them. When it was clear to Beatrice how badly he wanted them to leave, she signaled Salai, and Salai shook the sack. The sack made the unmistakable sound of gold on gold, and that helped the merchant to decide that he would allow them to look around. Nothing washes cleaner than gold.

"How much for this saltcellar?" Beatrice asked.

The silversmith reached over her shoulders, taking the piece from her grasp. "Forty ducats," he said, sniffing into his perfumed handkerchief. "The Duchess of Milan herself has one just like it."

Beatrice looked at Salai and asked, "Have you seen such at the castle?"

Salai shook his head no.

"Only yesterday," the merchant said, "one of our duchess' agents came to my shop to inquire about purchasing several of my wares for her collections. It is an honor to be asked to serve our lady's exquisite taste."

"Would it be worth ten ducats to serve her exquisite taste?"

"It is worth much more than that," the merchant replied.

Beatrice turned to Salai and said, "We're going to buy a saltcellar." Salai grinned broadly and bobbed his head up and down as he had seen the court jesters do. He then reached into his sack and brought forth the ten fish. He laid them out on the counter one by one, looking up at Beatrice and waiting for her nod before laying down the next. The merchant coughed and sputtered and urged Salai to hurry up and get to the money, but Salai took his time. He placed a gold ducat on each fish, wiping the coin on his shirt first, looking up to Beatrice and smiling before placing it so. Once each fish had a single coin, he repeated the process with a second. Beatrice smiled at the merchant. "The fish help him count," she said after Salai had laid out a total of thirty ducats.

"Your boy is not finished. He must lay one more coin on each fish. Four coins times ten fish equals forty coins."

Beatrice said, "That cannot be. Three apples times ten pears is thirty apple-pears. Therefore, four coins times ten fish is equal to forty fish-coins or coin-fish, whichever you prefer."

The merchant said, "No, you see, these fish are merely counters."

"No," Beatrice said, "that cannot be either—the fish are *on* the counter." Salai did his best not to smile.

The silversmith shook his head to clear it, then said, "The price of the saltcellar is forty ducats. I have nothing more to add."

"I don't want you to add," Beatrice said. "I want you to subtract. You said that it was worth ten ducats to serve the Duchess of Milan. Forty subtract ten equals thirty." Then Beatrice smiled at him, looked down at her toes and said softy, shyly, "I am the Duchess of Milan."

The shopkeeper's patience was at its absolute end. He

decided that he had had enough. He looked across his shop and saw the handsome and well-dressed San Severino and Francesco walk in. In a voice loud enough for San Severino, Francesco and half of Milan to hear, the merchant said, "If you are the Duchess of Milan, I must say that the Duke of Milan is Neptune himself, for you smell like a fishwife."

At that moment Beatrice sent a signal to San Severino, and he came bounding over. He kissed her heartily on both cheeks. "How are you, my fair duchess?" he asked. Francesco followed suit. He, too, came over, bowed and greeted Beatrice according to the custom of the court. The merchant smiled and stammered, confused and worried that he had not only lost a sale but also lost the chance to serve the Duchess of Milan.

Beatrice, San Severino and Francesco all linked arms together and were about to leave the shop when Beatrice turned and said to Salai, "Please give the man forty ducats. The saltcellar is certainly worth only thirty, but the afternoon's entertainment is worth ten." Salai quickly placed one more ducat on each fish. Beatrice then picked up the saltcellar and said to the silversmith, "I have made an honest man of you, sir. Now you can tell the world that the Duchess of Milan has a saltcellar just like this."

Salai glanced over at the row of fish, each one having four gold ducats laid on it. "I'll leave you my fishies," he said. And then they all linked arms and marched out.

That evening they told of the day's happening, Salai

miming both the role of buyer and seller and San Severino narrating.

Craftsmen, poets, artists soon flooded to the court of Milan. Those who came because of money stayed because they were enchanted. Money alone could not explain why the clavichord, all ebony and ivory, that Lorenzo da Pavia built for Beatrice was the most beautiful in the world. Nor could it explain why Master Sorba, the Spanish embroiderer, designed gowns and capes for her that were finer than any he had done for other duchesses, including Beatrice's own mother. And the goldsmith Carodosso had been employed by Il Moro before, but it was after he met Beatrice that he designed the famous rope of pearls and diamonds to which he added the priceless ruby known as El Spigo. All produced their finest works, for the young Duchess of Milan had an invisible measuring rod in her head. Everyone employed by her knew that he was not in competition with other craftsmen; he was in competition with perfection.

Salai, too, offered the young duchess the best fruits of his labors. He stole a Turkish hide from Leonardo and instead of giving it to his father as he had planned, sold it, and with the money he purchased the very finest anise comfits and gave them to Beatrice.

There was no one more alive to beauty than Beatrice, and there was no one more alive to Beatrice than Salai.

TIME AND AGAIN when Il Moro sought Leonardo to ask his advice about engineering or war machines or the design of the castle walls, he found the master with Beatrice discussing art or playing his lute and singing for her. Il Moro came to his wife's çhambers seeking Leonardo, but he stayed because he, too, became enchanted. Smart, happy talk and laughter permeated the air. Surely if this small dark thing could interest a giant intellect like Leonardo, surely if this young plain girl could inspire men to lift their crafts into the realm of art, then surely there must be something there that he had not seen. So Il Moro, who had used

Leonardo's eyes to investigate the course of rivers and to improve the plan of cities, now used Leonardo's eyes to discover his very own wife.

Il Moro decided to accompany Beatrice to Vigevano, her favorite country home. Leonardo had gone there to develop some plans he had for improving the vineyards and for irrigating the land. After he arrived, the duke set Leonardo to begin construction of a model village. Work began to spill over into the evenings. Salai resented having chores that kept him from Beatrice. "What has happened to Il Moro?" he asked. "He has us working on a dozen things all at once. What's wrong with having only the usual half a dozen? What is wrong with that guy?"

"There's nothing wrong with Ludovico," Leonardo answered. "He is in love. Love makes a lazy man lazier and an ambitious one even more ambitious."

"Well, who is our dear duke in love with this time?" Salai asked.

"Our dear duke is in love with our dear duchess."

Salai swallowed hard. He knew who the duke was in love with this time. He had seen the duke's love happen. "Yeah?" he said, "Who does he think he is, falling in love with his wife. We discovered her first."

One evening during their stay at Vigevano Leonardo was called to the duke's chambers. Duchess Beatrice was there too. Salai accompanied Leonardo, hoping for an evening of talk and games, but Il Moro wanted to discuss business. They finished discussing plans for the model farm when Ludovico cleared his throat, a well-known mark of punctuation at the court of Milan. "Master Leonardo," he began, "I would like you to do a portrait of my beloved wife. Only you can capture her beauty and put it down properly. I would like you to begin it tomorrow, here at Vigevano. From our ride over the grounds today, I can see that your work on the vineyards and the farm has progressed enough to allow time for this work of art."

Salai, deprived of his games and his time with Beatrice, thought, what does he expect Leonardo to do? Grow a tail and paint with that? The duke had already given him enough work for both hands. But, Salai thought, if Leonardo does begin to paint Beatrice, it would give them many hours when she could sit, and he, Salai, could look at her, talk to her and keep her amused.

Salai's thoughts were just beginning to brighten when he heard Beatrice say, "But certainly, my husband, Master Leonardo cannot begin to paint in Vigevano when all of his tools are in Milan."

"I will send for them," Il Moro said. "Make me a list, Master Leonardo. They will be here the day after tomorrow. You may begin then."

"Dear husband," Beatrice said, "I know why you want

me to sit for my portrait. I am becoming such an excellent horsewoman and so superb at falconing that you are getting extremely jealous. You want nothing more than for me to stop improving my horsemanship and sit still. I'll tell you what. I will have my portrait done by Master Leonardo only if you allow me to be painted astride my horse."

"But, Beatrice, dear wife, no lady is ever portrayed in such manner. Sitting upon a horse is suitable for conquering warriors, not for gentle and sweet wives."

"Are you worried, dear Moro, that people looking at my portrait will not know which is the horse and which is the wife?"

"Now, now, Beatrice, you are making sport with me."

"Not at all. If Master Leonardo can do a portrait of an ermine with the same pose as Madonna Cecilia Gallerani, I thought that he could do a portrait of a horse with the same pose as me. A horse suits me better."

There was a pause, a long pause. Il Moro looked from his wife to Leonardo and then to the floor. "You are too much of a tease," he said.

Beatrice advanced toward her husband. "Look at me, Ludovico," she said. He raised his eyes from the floor. When their eyes met, Beatrice began to laugh. She threw her head back and laughed until ripples of sound crisscrossed the room. Il Moro looked first confused and then relaxed and then he, too, started to laugh. Salai, taking his cue from his duke and duchess, tried to force great guffaws from his throat, but he could not. He had heard Beatrice's genuine laughter so often that he knew this was mere sound. Leonardo remained solemn.

Beatrice stopped laughing suddenly, suddenly before Il Moro realized that she had done so; his continuing laughter rang hollow and harsh. Then he, too, stopped, and Leonardo tugged at Salai's collar as a signal for them to leave. Salai recognized the look, frozen and withdrawn, on his master's face. It was the look he always wore when human emotions became too intense or too raw.

Salai never learned what Beatrice said to Ludovico after they left, but he noticed that Leonardo's paints were not sent for the next day or the next. He also noticed that when they returned to Milan, Cecilia Gallerani had gotten married to Count Bergamini and left the castle, taking her portrait with her.

LATE in the month of their third January together, Beatrice gave birth to their first baby. The child was as little and as much as Ludovico had wanted: a boy. In celebration he caused the bells to ring for six days, and he set free all the people who were in prison for debts. They first called their little boy Ercole, after Beatrice's father, and Beatrice's father was proud. But they changed the young man's name to Maximilian, after the Holy Roman Emperor; that made the Emperor Maximilian proud. And that was better politically.

Ludovico could not cease praising his wife. He displayed his affection for her openly, and Beatrice blossomed. Watching her flowering within these few years was as dramatic as seeing the whole of a lifetime condensed into a few hours upon a stage. There was not a person in the court of Milan who was not in love with the young, vivacious duchess. And there was not a person more in love with her than the thirteen-year-old Salai. Beatrice was now in full control as wife, mother and duchess. Her duties occupied many hours, but her free time was always available to Salai. He had moved from full-time to part-time occupant in her life. But the hours that they shared together were shared completely.

Everything he saw he examined for some way to gain Beatrice's attention. When he saw Leonardo turn an idle doodle into a pattern and then a design, Salai took the page and presented it to Beatrice. "I thought," he said, "that you might like this design to decorate a sleeve, my lady."

"Is this your work, Salai?"

"I commissioned it from Master Leonardo."

Beatrice studied the page. She turned it over and upside down and sideways. "Thank you very much, Salai. But are you certain that Leonardo does not need the drawing of the horse that is here on the left?"

"I am sick of the horse, my lady."

"Did you steal this design from Master Leonardo, Salai?" Beatrice asked.

"I never steal, my lady. Do you consider it stealing to take milk from a cow in order to make a pudding?"

"All right, Salai," Beatrice said. "I shall make a pudding." She gave the design to Sorba, the Spanish embroiderer, and Sorba used it on the sleeve of her gown.

The Duchess Isabella came to visit her sister and her new nephew in March. "Oh, Beatrice, dear sister," Isabella exclaimed, "how you have ripened like a good Milano cheese."

"Thank you, Isabella. And you, dear sister, have polished your glow. You are even more lovely."

"Perhaps she is more lovely because there *is* more," Salai suggested. He noticed that Isabella was getting fat.

Isabella made her way to the nursery, where she saw Maximilian in his cradle. "Oh!" she said, and then followed it with "Aaaah! It is taking all my strength of will not to reach into that cradle and pick him up in my arms," she said.

"Oh, sister, please do," Beatrice urged. She herself reached into the covers and lifted up her son and gently handed him over to Isabella.

"Aaaah!" Isabella said. "One feels close to God when one holds an infant." Whereupon she immediately handed him over to his nurse, saying, "They always spit up on me."

"I thought you liked good Milano cheese," Salai said.

"Who is this young man?" Isabella asked her sister.

"Salai," Beatrice answered. "He is assistant to Master Leonardo da Vinci."

"Oh, so the master is still with you. I wondered if he still were. I have received no word about a work I had asked for. I wondered what happened to my bust of the young Christ."

"The model developed a nasty tongue and the beginnings of a beard," Salai said.

Isabella squinted at Salai.

Beatrice broke into the awkwardness of the moment, saying, "Salai, why don't you show Duchess Isabella about the castle. Show her the theater we have had built."

Salai was happy to do as Beatrice had asked.

What a strange thing is a sister, he thought. He had a sister, but his Dorotea was as different from Isabella as plain is different from fancy. Dorotea could never have what he had, yet the more fortune smiled upon him, the more Dorotea did too. She never stopped bragging to her friends about her beautiful brother. And Salai never stopped trying to do for her. He stole a silverpoint from Boltraffio and gave her the money he got for it. He brought her bits of cloth and gossip, and with these she purchased prestige among her friends. Theirs was an exchange, not a competition.

Salai knew that showing Isabella around the castle would provide him with a wonderful chance to tease. He also knew that to make the teasing stick, he must first flatter. Like applying sizing to a canvas to make it accept the paint. "Master Leonardo himself," he began, "wanted to escort the Duchess Isabella. He regrets that he cannot. So he sent me—poor excuse for a guide though I am—instead. I shall attend to you and show you everything, or I shall have Master Leonardo to answer to. The master remembers with joy your last visit to his studio. He has told me that since you made an appearance there the light from the north window is brighter and clearer."

Isabella linked her arm through Salai's. "As we walk you may tell me what else Master Leonardo has said."

Salai took Isabella first to the theater that Il Moro had built for his wife. Then to the room of the baby gifts, where two soldiers stood guard day and night. Then to the room where Beatrice displayed her collections: one cabinet full of Murano glass and another full of ivories, another of swords inlaid with gold and jewels. Then to the room of musical instruments. "It is very much," Isabella muttered. She walked over to the clavichord on which Lorenzo da Pavia had lavished love and talent and skill. All around it were mottoes in Greek and Latin, ivory-inlaid into the ebony. The clavichord was so beautiful that Isabella stopped short and caught her breath before she said, most coolly, "It pays to be plain. My sister is as a blank sheet of parchment to works of art. Everyone chooses to add a stroke of decoration."

When Salai showed her the wardrobes of gowns, she said, "One would think she is in a vestry looking at the robes of the Pope and his bishops. I've never seen so many gowns."

Salai pulled out the dress with the braid on the sleeve, the braid done from the design of Leonardo. "The master designed this sleeve for our duchess."

"Master Leonardo da Vinci?"

Salai nodded. "The same."

Salai next guided Isabella to the bathroom. He opened the door and exclaimed, "Behold!"

"I shall not enter," Isabella declared.

"You must, my lady," Salai implored. "Come see. The master did this, too. He engineered the whole thing. It was our gift to our duchess."

"How quaint."

"No, not quaint. Practical. Come see." He pushed Isabella toward the center of the room.

"Warm in here," she said, fanning herself with her hand.

Salai clapped his hands. "That's it! That's it! Master Leonardo designed it. The heat comes from a hidden closet and is piped all over the room, so our duchess will not catch a chill when she gets out of her bath. The master designed it, and I have named it. I call it central heating."

Isabella turned to Salai with a furious look on her face.

"Take me to Master Leonardo," she demanded.

"He is at work on the horse."

"My sister has the talent of all of Italy at her call, and she uses that of Leonardo da Vinci for bathrooms and dress sleeves. What a waste," Isabella moaned. "There is certainly in Italy some subject more fit for Master Leonardo's talents than designing braid and bathrooms. I can think of a very good subject for his brush," she said, lifting her chin and gazing off into the distance, posing.

"Oh," Salai explained. "Duchess Beatrice does not choose to have her portrait painted by Leonardo."

"Beatrice is not who I had in mind," Isabella said. She lifted her chin and posed again. "Beatrice is not who I had in mind at all," she repeated. That ended the tour.

There were many people at the court of Milan who thought that Isabella was brilliant; she was clever, and she was spoiled, and she was titled, and to the many people who depended on court patronage, that passed for brilliance. Isabella, who for years had been the family star, the beloved bride, the cultured leader of Mantua, suffered for attention in Milan. There were those fawning courtiers, the grackles, the Francesco crowd, always willing to flatter, but it was not they whom she wanted to attract. It was the intellectuals, the gifted, the skilled craftsmen whose favor she wanted; the very elements who were drawn naturally to Beatrice, the small, dark, accepting sister, the one with the invisible but true measuring rod in her head, the sister who collected, not the sister who accumulated.

One evening in April, in that year 1493 when Isabella's stay was already a month old, she made another attempt to capture the minds of the intellects. She read to the small group gathered in her sister's chambers a letter that had been forwarded to her from Mantua. She said that it had been written by Ponzone, a scholar friend of hers. Had no one ever heard of Ponzone? Why! in Mantua he was consulted about everything from childbirth to menus. "Oh," Salai said, "our duke has an astrologer too." "Master Ponzone reads books, not bird droppings," Isabella said scornfully as she unfolded the paper and read it out:

I hear that a man named Columbus lately discovered an island for the King of Spain, on which are men of our height but of copper-colored skin, with noses like apes. The chiefs wear a plate of gold in their nostrils which covers the mouth, the men and women alike. Twelve men and four women have been brought back to the King of Spain, but they are so weakly that two of them fell ill of some sickness which the doctors do not understand, and they had no pulse and are dead. The others have been clothed, and if they see any one who is richly clad they stroke him with their hands and kiss his hands to show how much they admire him. They seem intelligent, and are very tame and gentle. No one can understand their language. They eat of everything at table, but are not given wine. In their own country they eat the roots of trees and some big kind of nut which is like pepper but yields good food, and on this they live."

"That is very interesting," Salai said. "I would like very

much to take the letter to Master Leonardo. He is interested in such things and likes to copy them into his notebooks."

Isabella was pleased that Leonardo would be interested in something that she had brought to his attention. That had been the purpose of her reading. She lent the letter to Salai after again listing Ponzone's credentials and after Salai gave her many reassurances that the letter would be returned whole and unblemished. "I will make certain that Master Leonardo does not make any of his famous scribbles on it."

"Oh?" Isabella said, "If the master chooses to scribble, as you call it, don't stop him."

"Oh, my lady, I will. I would not want your famous Ponzone's letter all cluttered with heads of the Virgin or some of the master's studies of nudes. Such things are not fit for the duchess' fair eyes."

"You let me be the judge of what is fit for my eyes."

"Your famous Ponzone's letter will be returned unblemished. There will be no studies of horses or of hands or of the infant Christ in the margins."

Isabella forced a smile. "Just see that the letter is returned to me, Salai."

Salai carried the letter to Leonardo, laughing. "Hey, boss!" he said. "Look what Isabella has done this time. She has invented a whole new world and someone named

Columbus to discover it, and someone named Ponzone to write her about it."

Leonardo read the letter and chuckled. He never copied it into his notebook. Salai knew he would not.

SALAI missed Isabella after she left; it was like losing both the player and the audience. In the weeks that followed he and Beatrice often shared again the events of Isabella's visit. Beatrice never began such a discussion; Salai always did, and he did so eagerly. He could do a complete imitation of Isabella's conversation with Lorenzo da Pavia, the maker of musical instruments. He would take both parts, switching chairs and voices as he became first Isabella asking for a clavichord and then Lorenzo refusing.

He missed Isabella as a source of material for his comic act. He came to look back on her visit as the climax of something shared between Beatrice and him as a view is shared by two people alone on a mountaintop, seeing the whole and seeing it the same.

Following the birth of little Maximilian, Il Moro added a large measure of pride to his love for his young wife. By the following May that pride had grown into admiration, and he decided to send Beatrice to Venice as his personal ambassador. Both Milan and Venice were wealthy and powerful; they had been rivals for many years. At times that rivalry had flared into warfare. Now, however, Ludovico considered it necessary that Venice become his ally because the King of France was threatening to invade Italy. The threat was a more immediate danger to Milan than to Venice. Il Moro knew that he needed peace on his right before he could make successful war on his left. So he decided to send Beatrice to Venice. She would be his representative. She could, he was certain, beguile even his own old worst enemy and make Venice the friend of Milan.

Beatrice was thrilled to be chosen as her husband's ambassador. She announced to Salai that she would be accompanied by her mother and an entourage of five hundred.

Salai reported the progress of preparations to Leonardo. "Today Beatrice's mother learned that each of the Milanese ladies will wear a long gold chain worth two hundred ducats, so Madama has supplied each of the ladies of Ferrara with a chain worth two hundred and twenty ducats."

Later Salai reported, "Beatrice has given some of her ladies strings of pearls for their paternosters, so Madama has given some of her ladies rosaries made of larger pearls still. Now Ludovico has decided that not *some* but *all* of our Milanese ladies should have pearl rosaries."

Only a few days passed before Salai again reported, "Beatrice's mother has given some of her smaller pendants to her ladies and has had gowns of green satin with broad stripes of black velvet made for all of them, so our Beatrice has sent for Caradosso, the goldsmith, and ordered him to bring an emergency supply of rubies and diamonds. She is having them strung into necklaces for the ladies of Milan. Beatrice hardly has time for anything but standing for fittings for her new gowns. At last count it will take ten chariots and fifty mules to carry her belongings." Salai realized that his idol, his Beatrice, was reacting to her mother more like a duchess than a daughter.

"Does she think she will impress her mother most if she is more like Isabella than like Beatrice?" he asked.

Leonardo laid down his notebook. "Our Duchess Beatrice does not want to impress her mother, Salai; she wants to hurt her. She wants to show her mother that she should not have neglected her poor, plain second daughter. She now thinks she can do battle with a weapon sharper than a sword. She's discovered that wealth can buy not only pleasure but also pain. Beatrice will use her money to try to cut out old wounds. It will be a while, Salai, before your dear friend Beatrice learns that the past is never entirely quiet within us. It will be a longer time still before she learns that the only way to conquer an unhappy past is to learn to live with it."

"If my past had been unhappy," Salai replied, "I would have been able to smother it with anise cookies alone."

"Some, even many, would consider that your past was unhappy."

"Not me. I wouldn't say that. I just say, 'What was, was; what is, is; what will be, will be.' Why can't Beatrice do that?"

Leonardo shook his head. "Some of us simply cannot. Some of us have to strain all of our present actions through past pain. Others of us merely learn to coat bad thoughts with silence and good manners. Not everyone can be a Salai." Leonardo then placed his hands on his chair and pushed himself up. "Anyway, Salai, it will be a while before your old friend is your old friend again. And perhaps it is good that our duchess shall have less need of you, for I shall have more. Besides finishing the horse, Il Moro has asked me to paint the end wall of the refectory of St. Maria delle Grazie. I suggested to him that our Lord's Last Supper would be an appropriate work to put on a wall the monks will face as they dine."

AFTER BEATRICE returned from Venice Salai kept track of all her activities. She was acquiring more gowns and more jewelry. Her collections of glass and silver and musical instruments grew. Her gowns grew fancier. Her confidence grew. Her conversation and her laughter grew louder. Everything grew, and she outgrew her need for Salai.

Salai missed her, missed what they had had between them. It was inevitable that what they had had between them would become stretched thin as each took up a firmer footing in life. Beatrice outgrew her need for Salai before he outgrew his for her; that, too, was bound to happen. What they had between them was a bond whose threads were spun in childhood. Those threads were stretched as their positions moved farther apart, as their ages dragged them farther and deeper into their life roles. Beatrice moved farther and faster because she was older and was Beatrice. Salai lagged partly because he was younger and mostly because he was Salai. He was never anxious to nudge the future.

Salai had done some growing up. He had put his childish thefts behind him. He had stopped stealing silverpoints and money and Turkish leather hides. But he had not stopped stealing. What he stole now were ideas, Leonardo's ideas, those thoughts that burst like star sparkle in all directions from the master's incandescent mind.

Leonardo could not have a thought without putting it down on paper. How to draw a pair of hands. How to show the folds of a gown. How to arrange a group of people. It was those ideas that Leonardo sketched, and Salai's new business was this: he would borrow those sketches from the studio and sell them to church artists and to artists in other workshops. Milan was full of people who had skill to draw or to paint, to fill in the lines, but who did not have Leonardo's eye to see something new or to see something old in a new way. All over Milan there began to appear works in the manner of Leonardo da Vinci, pale imitations that had the characteristics but not the character of the master's work.

Salai never thought of his new enterprise as stealing. It

was a rental business. He always shared his profits with Dorotea and with his father, who was now an invalid. And he almost always returned the used sketches. Salai still could not regard the ideas of others as personal or as property.

In November, following Beatrice's trip to Venice, Ludovico Il Moro's niece married Maximilian, the Holy Roman Emperor. Il Moro wished to have all his worldly goods displayed and all his worldly friends impressed. He requested that Leonardo construct a model of the horse. At last Leonardo made a clay form out of ten years' worth of study.

The horse stood twenty-six feet high, the largest statue of a horse ever attempted. It took tons of clay and of steel reinforcements to make.

Salai, who loved the stupendous, loved the horse. He thought that Il Moro had chosen a wise way to impress the visitors to Milan. "Well, boss," he said, "that is the biggest, best horse I have ever seen. It's the biggest, best horse anyone has ever seen. To cast it will take enough bronze to make cannon for a whole army."

Leonardo, who loved to astound, loved the horse. "That it will take much bronze is a worry, Salai. The duke has promised me the bronze before Christmas. I shall be ready to cast it, and I shall be ready not to. There is always the possibility that the duke will have to make a choice. If he must choose between honoring the memory of his father with a bronze horse or fighting for his honor with bronze cannon, I know which he will choose." Leonardo looked at his creation, muzzle to hoof, hock and fetlock. He stroked its underbelly, smiling.

Before the horse was moved to the castle courtyard, Beatrice came to see it. Salai was delighted. He had not visited with her for a while. Sometimes weeks now passed without their seeing each other, but they were always glad when they did. Sometimes it took a minute or two before there appeared the flash of their former selves, a flash of the joke shared between them.

Beatrice studied the horse a long, long time. Salai followed her gaze eagerly, expectantly. She said nothing. She walked around the monument slowly, looking slowly. Finally, Salai could stand it no longer. "Well!" he burst out, "isn't that the greatest damn horse you have ever seen?"

"Yes," Beatrice answered. "It is great in that it is large. I would guess that it is the largest model of a horse ever made in Milan or anywhere."

"You bet," Salai replied.

"It will serve its purpose. Whereas delicacy impresses the French, largeness always impresses the Germans. Maximilian will love it."

"What's the matter with you? Don't you love it too?"

"No, I don't love it," Beatrice answered. She looked over at Salai. "I am sorry that I do not. I wanted very much to love it."

Salai said nothing. What was the matter with her? Had her head become too filled with dresses and jewelry? Had gewgaws crowded out that great measuring rod by which she always knew the good from the mediocre and the great from the good?

"The horse is not the master's best," Beatrice continued. "It is not so much a work of art as it is a *labor* of art. I think Messer Leonardo impresses more when he tries less. One cannot look at the horse and keep from seeing the effort that has gone into it. A person looking at a work of art should not be slapped to attention; he should be wooed."

"You would never have said that three years ago."

"That is true. I never would have said it three years ago, but I would have thought it. Three years ago I would not have told you what I am about to tell you now. Listen to me," she said. "Listen now, Salai. We have not nearly enough time to talk anymore, and I want to tell you this." She paused and riveted her eyes on her young friend. "Your master Leonardo needs something from you. He needs your rudeness and your irresponsibility."

"I think I've come a long way—" Salai protested.

"You have. You have. Let's not waste time arguing. I'm

trying to tell you that you must not go all the way. If you ever become totally tame, Leonardo will have no need of you."

Salai smiled. "Please continue."

Beatrice returned his smile, relaxed at his reaction. "It is no mystery to me why Leonardo has put up with your stealing and why he puts up with your selling his ideas." Salai gasped when she said this; Beatrice shook her head. "I know all about it, Salai, and I'm sure that somewhere in that monumental mind of Leonardo's is an awareness of what you are doing." She looked up at the horse momentarily, then she looked at Salai a long time before she continued. "He needs a wild element," she said at last. "All great art needs it: something that leaps and flickers. Some artists can put that wild element into the treatment itself, but Leonardo cannot. He is too self-conscious. When he has an important commission from an important client on an important subject, he ties up all his instincts. He strives, not to let himself go, but to be perfect. Even in outline, the work on the wall of the refectory has the beginnings of greatness in it. The audience, a poor bunch of monks, is not important, and Leonardo has allowed his mind to idle a little and let in something fresh and wild. Salai, I ask you to see to it that Master Leonardo keeps something wild, something irresponsible in his work."

Salai was quiet. He allowed her thinking to sink in, and

then he asked, "What shall I tell the master? He will not directly ask your opinion, but he is certain to hint that he wants to know."

"Tell Leonardo da Vinci that the Duchess of Milan congratulates him on giving form to tons of chalk."

"Mountains also give form to tons of chalk."

"Well, that's all right. God gave form to that chalk. Leonardo will not mind being classed with God. It is only when he feels that he is no man to match mountains that he is plunged into melancholy."

Salai studied the horse a long while. Then he focused on Beatrice. "Is that why you will not have the master paint your portrait? Are you afraid that you are too important a client, too important a subject and too important an audience? Are you afraid that his treatment of you will be too heavy?"

"That is only part of the reason."

"What would you have the master do for you, my lady?"

"He has already done it. He has shown my husband that I am worthy of his love." Beatrice paused a minute. "I am grateful to Leonardo for that. For showing Il Moro the interesting whorl of leaves beneath the plain flower of my face. You must keep my thoughts about the horse to yourself, Salai. That great mound of talent and intellect called Leonardo da Vinci has a very thin skin. Very thin. He deflates at the tiniest prick."

Beatrice left, waving goodbye to Salai and saluting him with a wink. Salai was left alone with the chalk horse and with his thoughts.

So Beatrice thought that the horse was great in size only. It lacked an element that raises a work of art from good to great. Something wild. Something that leaps and flickers. Like lightning? Leonardo had called the festivals lightning. They were altogether wild, and the horse was altogether refined, and neither was great. A great work needed a sense of the important touched with something wild. Beatrice ought to be listened to; she had not lost that invisible measuring rod in her head.

Beatrice was asking Salai to be responsible for Leonardo's keeping something wild in his work. She also told Salai what his street urchin instincts had told him long ago: that Leonardo da Vinci needed him, the untalented, rude, irresponsible Salai; that he was completing Leonardo da Vinci. Beatrice had put words to it.

He wished she had not. He didn't want the words; he didn't want to be responsible for Leonardo. He had his father and Dorotea, and that was enough. Enough. Of course, his responsibility for them was much less serious. Whatever he did for them changed only the outside of their lives. Giving them money was not helping something that was inside them.

For all these years Salai had understood his role, but he

had always avoided its definition. But now Beatrice had put words to it. She had charged Salai with (dreaded word, more dreaded thought) *responsibility*. And worse, she had made him responsible for being wild, for being, in effect, irresponsible.

S ALAI saw even less of Beatrice in the months
following the completion of the clay horse, the
months when Leonardo continued working on the
wall of the refectory. Most of Salai's knowledge of Beatrice was now official news. They almost never had private
meetings. She was busy being wife and mother and diplo-
mat.

He learned that the King of France came on a visit, and
Beatrice danced for him, and Il Moro was pleased. A second
son was born to Beatrice, and of the fifteen names the child
received at his baptism, they chose to call him Francesco.
Il Moro was pleased. She continued to amuse her husband.

She had shown him the world as a theater, and he continued enjoying her performance.

Every now and then as she was going to or coming from the chapel of St. Maria delle Grazie, and as Salai was going to or coming from its refectory, they would exchange a few words.

"On what is our Lord now feasting?" she would ask.

"Judas has just spilled the salt," he would call back. Or another time he would answer, "St. Peter has just finished whispering into his neighbor's ear." Salai always enjoyed these brief encounters.

There were days when Leonardo would stand from dawn to dusk on the platform before the *Last Supper*. On those days the master would work furiously, never laying down his brush or stopping to eat or drink. Then three or four days could pass, and he would not touch the wall at all. Instead he would sit and look at it for an uninterrupted hour or two. There were other days when he would take Salai with him to the courtyard, where he continued working on preparations to cast the horse in bronze, and he would suddenly leave and race over to the refectory, where he would add a dab or two to the wall and then rush back to pick up again his work on the horse.

Leonardo's habits did not allow the usual procedures for fresco. Usually the entire wall was prepared with a rough plaster. Then an assistant laid down fine plaster, in the amount that the artist could finish in a single day. The artist would apply his colors to the wet plaster; the colors dissolved in the plaster, and when it dried and hardened, the color, the painting became part of the plaster. Once laid down, the colors and their shapes could not be scraped off and could not be changed.

But Leonardo never chose to work fast. Time was his enemy, and he never wanted to be at its mercy, so Leonardo had prepared the wall in the refectory by sealing it with mastic and varnish, a mixture of his own invention, to keep salts and moisture of the walls from seeping through.

Leonardo's notebooks had become filled with faces and poses. He had chosen to paint the moment when Christ said to his disciples, "One of you will betray me." And he had wanted the look and the pose of each of the twelve disciples to expose the man's character. Leonardo had walked the streets of Milan looking for faces that could represent St. Peter or St. John or Thomas or James.

When the prior had complained to Il Moro that Leonardo's work was taking too long and that his monks needed their refectory, Il Moro had passed the complaint along. Leonardo had answered, "Tell the prior that I have not yet found a face to serve as a model for Judas, but I am becoming convinced that his will do." Il Moro had been amused at Leonardo's reply and repeated it to everyone at court.

Even two major projects, the *Last Supper* and the horse, were not enough to occupy all of Leonardo's mind; some part was always searching. He said to Salai one day, "I understand that the people of Flanders skim across the ice by attaching the bones of animals to their boots. Please send a message to Benedetto Portinari that I would like to talk to him; he has just returned from Flanders. He can tell me which bones."

Salai, aware that he had sold one of Leonardo's sketches to an artist employed by Mr. Portinari, objected, "Oh, boss, why waste your good time with a dull man of business?"

"Mr. Portinari is the least dull of businessmen, Salai. Summon him."

"I'll find out for you and bring back the information instead of Portinari."

"I want to talk to the man. Now go. Arrange a meeting."

Salai hoped to catch Portinari while he was busy, too busy to answer a message from Leonardo. Salai watched the merchant's house a whole morning. He saw four men enter and he waited a quarter of an hour after that before approaching the door and asking to see Mr. Portinari.

"Messer Portinari is in conference," the servant said. "Who shall I say wants him?"

Salai never ceased enjoying the effect he had on his fellow servants when he mentioned the name of his master.

He recognized that servants of the lowly were regarded as lowly. He knew that he need only drop the name of his master to raise himself higher than this fellow at the door. "I am sent by my master, Leonardo da Vinci."

"Oh, yes. Master Leonardo. Oh, yes. Yes. Certainly. I will tell Master Portinari immediately."

The man disappeared for only a moment. He returned with Mr. Portinari at his side. The merchant rubbed his hands together. "Oh, yes. Yes," he said. "Tell your master that I shall be there immediately. Run." He turned back and glanced impatiently toward the room from which he had come. "I have only a small matter to attend to. Some men to dismiss. It will take me only a minute. Run along now, boy." He started to reenter his house when he turned back suddenly and smiled at Salai. He reached into his purse and handed him a coin. "Here," he said. "For you. I appreciate your bringing me the message."

Salai sauntered back to the workshop, thinking, flipping the coin. He knew that his career as a salesman of Leonardo's ideas would come to an end shortly. Very shortly. That very morning. He could see how Mr. Benedetto Portinari was going to love telling Master Leonardo da Vinci that he had long been an admirer of his and how a certain artist he knew had obtained a certain drawing of the master's and how that artist had made him a fine work in the style of the master. No masterpiece, certainly, but a fine work indeed. Faced with facts instead of suspicion, Leonardo would have to call a halt to Salai's business. Salai imagined the whole scene, and he laughed to himself. Amusement always filled the pockets of his brain before melancholy had a chance. Salai smiled as he thought of how eager the man, the rich merchant Portinari, was to meet the master face to face. If Portinari were so anxious, so would others be. He, Salai, could begin a new business. He could arrange audiences with Leonardo as bishops arranged them for the Pope. He would do it for the pompous instead of the pious. He would do it so that they could tell friends and relatives and strangers what the great mind of Leonardo had revealed to them.

Yes, he could do it.

Yes, he would do it.

For a price.

After Mr. Portinari left Leonardo's studio, Leonardo called in to him. "Close the door," he said. "There is something I must discuss with you. A matter of business."

Salai closed the door and walked over to his master. He was prepared to tell Leonardo that he would never again rent out the master's sketches. He was not only prepared to make a promise, he was also prepared to keep it. Small matter. He had already mentally listed the names of clients for his new enterprise, the selling of audiences.

THE MONTHS became space surrounded by a thin shell of years. Passing time was an adversary to Leonardo, but to Salai time was a container for events: some colored bright, others pale and a few dark. His father died. Dorotea needed his help more than ever, but that was a shallow responsibility, easily borne.

The times were strange. There was a worship of both art and war, a worship of both creation and destruction. And Master Leonardo da Vinci embodied both. Where, other than in the person of his own master, could someone find a man who could devise the most outrageous machines of war and in the same notebook, sometimes on the same page, create a tender picture of a mother and child?

Salai probably understood Leonardo better than anyone. He never searched for understanding; it came to him by observation and acceptance. He had an acceptance of people and situations and a sufficient lack of self importance to allow himself to observe any situation by blending into it. He could be solemn; he could be gay. He could be honest; he could be dishonest. He could be coarse; he could be well-mannered. He never had a particular self-image that he wanted to present.

But Leonardo did. Leonardo chose to set himself apart —above and apart. He was never comfortable when people and emotions got too close; a human situation could show him to be less than perfect.

Leonardo's need to be elevated before an audience combined with the general worship of art to make Salai's sale of audiences brisk and profitable. Salai regarded his profiting from this combination of the times with Leonardo's temperament as part of his obligation. To his master. To Beatrice. And to himself. His curls and his disposition remained sunny.

Threat of an invasion by France seemed more likely than ever. The bronze that had been promised to Leonardo to cast the horse was needed for cannon. Il Moro sent the metal to Beatrice's father, his ally.

Despite the threat of war, Beatrice had continued to accumulate jewels and gold and silver plate. The accumulation became so immense that it was stored in oak cupboards for which Leonardo had to design special locks. What had once been elegant and selective had now become merely vast. And Beatrice's manner of dress was now fancy and fussy.

Salai could not understand what had happened to his friend. He seldom saw her now; there were no opportunities for him to observe and to allow his instincts to lead him to an understanding. Why was she accumulating goods like a warehouse? Was she too tired to be selective? Why was she covering up her plain outer self with jewels and ribbons? Was she too tired to make her plainness invisible?

Late in the summer of 1496 Salai began to see Beatrice come often to the chapel of St. Marie delle Grazie. Whereas before it had been her habit to come for holy days, she was now making daily visits.

Leonardo was hard at work on the refectory wall; he had solved all the problems of composition and was now left with the job of making his idea take form, a job as much of hand as of mind.

One day in early autumn, as Salai saw Beatrice's carriage approach the chapel, he waited outside for her. When she emerged, he asked her in the name of their old friendship to allow him to show her the wall. Leonardo had quit work for the day, they would be alone, and he was anxious to know her private opinion. They had exchanged only the most casual remarks since that day of the horse. He wanted to know if Beatrice would consider the *Last Supper* a great work of art.

Beatrice stood before the wall a long time. She walked from left to right, from St. Bartholomew to St. Simon and back again from St. Simon across Saints John and Andrew to St. Bartholomew. She was deep in thought. Her thinking filled the room. Even the rustle of her gown and the clink of her necklaces seemed muffled by her thoughts. At last she spoke. "No one who sees this will ever be free of Leonardo's vision. From this time on every painter of the *Last Supper* will be a follower." She studied the wall further. "No one," she said, "can see this painting and be but different for having seen it."

Salai, who had been studying Beatrice as she had been studying the painting, said, "You are different, my lady."

"There! You see," Beatrice said, throwing up her hands in mock exasperation, "it has happened to me already."

"That is not the *different* I am referring to."

"Then you must be referring to my form. I am different. I am about to become a mother again."

"That, too, is not the difference I mean."

"I am older. Age makes a difference."

"I would say, my lady, that the difference is that Beatrice is not now happy and that she once was."

Beatrice, who had kept her eyes on the painting as they bantered, turned to her young friend. "How can you say that?"

"Your gaiety is too loud. And so is your dress. Both are covering up something."

Beatrice stared at Salai. He was now taller than she was, and she tilted her head up and fastened her eyes on his. He boldly answered her glare. At last she spoke, "You were more fun, Salai," she said, "before you learned to think." Then she lifted her gown, ever so slightly, and walked out of the refectory.

Il Moro, too, was impressed with Leonardo's work on the wall. The master returned from a meeting with the duke with a new vineyard and a new commission. The vineyard, a fine one outside the walls of Milan, was an expression of thanks. The commission was for a portrait. Il Moro requested that Leonardo paint one of Beatrice's maids, a certain Lucrezia Crivelli.

"When are you to start?" Salai asked.

"Tomorrow."

Salai accompanied Leonardo to Madonna Lucrezia's apartment. Duke Ludovico was there, waiting, smiling. When Salai saw how the duke looked at the young lady, he knew why Beatrice looked as she did; he knew why Beatrice's gowns had grown loud. His duchess was making a pitiful attempt to muffle the sounds of a heart in the process of breaking.

Ludovico pressed Leonardo to make short work of the portrait. "I do not want to find gray in her hair before it is finished," he said, running his hand affectionately over her smooth dark head.

Leonardo allowed Salai to paint in the background. He worked on modeling her face and ribbons. He allowed some of his other apprentices to add finishing touches to Lucrezia's hair and gown and jewelry. All was completed in short order.

Beatrice came to the studio one night and tapped at Salai's window. "I want to see it," she said.

Salai did not need to ask what; he led her to the portrait. She stepped back and raised her lamp and looked. She then stepped forward and traced a ribbon with her finger, almost absent-mindedly "The plumage looks brighter than the bird," she said. "I also think the plumage looks borrowed, like a chicken wearing the feathers of an ostrich. She will fade before her ribbons do. I can wait." She then turned from the painting and said, "You see, Salai, there are advantages to having had good lessons in being second choice."

"Leonardo hates fussiness in women's dresses. He had no appetite to paint her plumage. He allowed two of his apprentices to help dress her—gown and jewelry." Salai then pointed to the band over the lady's forehead. "I did that. How do you like it?"

"You have done an excellent job, Salai. Mona Lucrezia looks like a very well-dressed, mildly intelligent cow."

"Why don't you let the master paint your portrait? You would be such a challenge, my lady. Leonardo loves to paint faces that reveal the soul, and all your beauty is inside."

Beatrice smiled, a smile both warm and knowing and cold and knowing. "I will not have him do my portrait," she said. "Instead I would have him paint me an arbor of green. In the dead of winter then, I shall have the central-heated bathroom to warm my body and the bower of spring green to warm my soul."

"What will you do about Mona Lucrezia?" Salai asked.

"I shall attend dances and the theater. And I shall play games with my children. I shall be very, very gay. And I shall pretend that I do not mind being second. That, Salai, is what I do best."

FOLLOWING that evening visit to the studio Beatrice began once again to invite Salai to her chambers in the evenings. Salai liked her as much as ever; their understanding and their ages had once again caught up with each other.

She now seemed to wear gaiety and cheerfulness more than she seemed to be them. She had sometimes to remind herself to laugh.

After she had seen the portrait of Lucrezia, Beatrice had simplified her dress, and Leonardo mentioned to Salai that he thought that their duchess was becoming beautiful. "She is beginning to have the look of layers," was the way he put it.

There was a habit of laughter among the three of them, and because Beatrice needed it, they kept that warm and lively. Beatrice made the Christmas season as gay as all her Christmases past. She gave Salai a bolt of velvet cloth to make into a cape, and he understood that there was enough for a gown for Dorotea. He gave to Beatrice a copy of one of Leonardo's drawings, one done by his own hand. He wanted her to have something that was as much like him as it could be. The drawing was that—an impious treatment of something very good. Beatrice accepted the drawing with a thank you and a smile. She did not comment on its artistic merit. Both of them knew it had none, and both of them knew that it was the thought between them that counted.

On Monday the second of January, the Duchess Beatrice went to church, waving and smiling at the people she passed in her chariot. She stopped in the studio and told Salai that there would be theater and dancing in her rooms that evening. "My husband, the duke, will attend, and I intend to dance quite a lot. The sight of me and this bobbing belly might remind my husband of what an entertaining creature I am."

The evening did not turn out that way at all.

At eight o'clock Beatrice was suddenly taken ill. Il Moro rushed to her side and carried her to her bedroom. Three hours later she gave birth to a dead baby boy, and an hour and a half after that—just as a new day began for all of

Milan—all the world ended for Beatrice, its duchess. She was twenty-two years old.

Salai sat stunned in the courtyard of the castle. He had just recovered his lady; they had only begun something newer and richer. He walked around the courtyard, trying to collect himself, trying to think of some way to break the news to Leonardo. At dawn he went to the studio. Leonardo was up, sitting at a desk, studying a book of mathematics.

Salai told him what had happened. Leonardo looked up from his book, but he did not look at the boy. He waited for Salai to finish, and then he resumed his reading, saying, "I have heard."

"What's the matter, Leonardo? You cannot say that you have heard. Didn't you understand? Our duchess is dead."

"I heard."

"Is that all you can say? *I heard.* Is that all she means to you?"

"Death is the ultimate product of life."

"How can you talk about death when I am talking about Beatrice? How can you talk about a process when I am talking about a person?"

"Do you expect me to shave my head and take all my meals standing?"

"No. Oh, Heaven forbid that you, you superhuman, Heaven forbid that you should care for someone more than you care for your work."

"I cared for Beatrice."

"You cared for Beatrice! You cared!" Salai screamed. "You care more for ideas than you care for people. You are a machine, Leonardo da Vinci. You are an idea machine. You are a frozen man, and all your paintings are frozen ideas, and you are a stiff, stuffy, conceited— You are nobody's friend— You aren't even—" Salai's voice grew louder and louder, and he began to choke on his own words.

It was then that Leonardo rose from his chair and guided the young man to bed.

THE GOOD fortune of Milan died with Beatrice.

Il Moro would not leave his room and he would not receive visitors. He fasted, and he shaved his head. After three days he emerged dressed in black, the color of his conscience. He continued to wear black, and he ate all his meals standing. He made rich contributions to the Church and to the hospitals. Every Monday and Thursday he shared a simple supper in the refectory with the Dominican brothers. There he looked upon the wall where Leonardo had frozen the moment, "One of you will betray me."

The French were making obvious their plans for invasion. Il Moro named Leonardo as chief engineer and assigned to him the job of studying the fortifications of the city.

Each day Leonardo left the studio before dawn; Salai heard his preparations to leave, but the boy stayed in bed until he heard the door close. Thus, both man and boy had time alone to recover from the outburst that had dampened their seven years together.

Salai would get up from bed with nothing to do. Doing nothing was suddenly difficult. It never had been difficult before. He had always conducted his own small business if he had no jobs to do for Leonardo. People were still willing to pay him for an introduction to Master Leonardo da Vinci, especially since the *Last Supper* had been completed. He could have made a nice income from the visitors from Florence alone. They came to Milan hungering after art; many of them could not be convinced that what was in Milan was better, but everyone of them would pay well to meet Leonardo. The Florentines were anxious to see him, if for no other reason than to carry home the notion that their men of genius were better. As if there were such a thing as a degree of genius. There were different kinds of genius, but there was no degree. *It* or *not it*. Salai could introduce no one to Leonardo these days. He was never in the studio, and Salai had lost his appetite for it.

Salai needed money as much as ever. Dorotea was planning to marry Carlo the blacksmith, and she needed a dowry.

Salai thought that perhaps now was the time to leave Leonardo. He could earn a living by making copies of the master's work. He could return home and open a small studio there. He could once again live the simple life that his father had lived and that Dorotea still did. He would welcome a life away from ideas, a life filled with good soup and bread and no questions needing answers.

He went home.

Dorotea stood when he entered the house. She always did; and as long as his father had had strength to do so, he had, too. Dorotea always served him first and best, even when his father was still alive. He had always enjoyed coming home to such treatment. But now that he had decided to stay forever, his sister's attitude made him feel awkward.

Carlo came for supper, and Salai and his sister's fiancé exchanged greetings. The young man remained standing and would not sit until Salai asked him to. Salai wanted to take an interest in his brother-in-law-to-be, so he asked him about his work.

"Do you think," Salai asked, "that the walk or the pace is the more natural for a horse?"

"Oh," Carlo answered, "I wouldn't never have give that some thought."

"Leonardo," Salai continued, "has been studying horses for some time now. He has concluded that the walk is the most natural."

"Well, I never, as I said, I never give that much thought at all. I just shods them as they bring them. I hardly notices anything above the hoof."

"Oh," Salai said.

They ate their supper in silence. The food was good. Good stew, simple spices, brewed a long time. Leonardo never ate meat. Home was, after all, where the food and the smells were familiar. And good. Of course the smells had changed since Salai had been bringing home money; Dorotea had cleaned the place up. Even so, the smells were familiar. Not quite as familiar as the smells of paint pots and glue, but they were good smells. All his senses, he decided, were comfortable: smell, taste, touch, hearing. Each was pleasing. Perhaps not the sound. He had grown to like the sound of the musicians that Leonardo hired to play in the studio. And, if he had to, he would admit that the sights of the studio were better. There was more color, more variety. But he could sacrifice some music and some art. Perhaps a little less of each was more comfortable. He could talk to these uncomplicated people about uncomplicated things.

"The duke is calling together a conference of artists and mathematicians for next month," he said.

The young blacksmith looked at Dorotea. "When he says *duke,* does he mean Il Moro?" he asked.

"Yes," Dorotea said proudly. "My brother lives close to the court."

Carlo said nothing for the rest of the evening, and Salai's talk soon tapered to the same. Anything, any commonplace thing he said had the ring of bragging to it. He didn't belong here. There were more pleasures than the simple pleasures of simple people, and he had grown to need them. He had outgrown home. He could no longer take on the simple, plain colors of his childhood.

He returned to the studio.

Leonardo decided to build a house on the grounds that Il Moro had given him. He asked Salai to oversee the project. Salai was amazed at how well suited he was for such a job. He could outshout and outswear the most vulgar workmen, and he made them get the job done. The swearing and the shouting served him well. He calmed down, and he once again accepted Leonardo's cool detachment about events that did not directly affect his person or his reputation.

Salai heaved brick and pounded lime and built inner strength as he built the house.

One evening he returned from the studio and found on the table by his bed a purse containing thirteen scudi. The note under the purse said "For Dorotea." The note was written in the mirror writing that was unmistakably Leonardo's.

THE FRENCH invasion came, and Il Moro and his children were forced to flee across the Alps into Germany. The duke left his city and its treasures to the rude French soldiers. They were a dirty lot. The French captains spit on the floors of the rooms, and the king himself had the habits of a sloth. A group of soldiers in the courtyard of the castle got drunk one night and used Leonardo's clay model of the horse as a great white target for their arrows. The horse, punctured in a hundred places, became a sponge for rainwater. It disintegrated, dissolved it would seem by tears sent from Heaven.

Leonardo and Salai left Milan. The whole world awaited them, and they chose Florence, the city from which Leonardo had come. Salai wanted to see Venice, the city that Beatrice had loved. Buildings faced with gold, streets of water, a bridge with shops on either side.

Leonardo agreed to go to Florence by way of Venice, but he also announced that they would stop at Mantua on the way. Isabella lived in Mantua, and Salai, who had never had much regard for her, had even less now that Beatrice was dead. What fun could Isabella be if Beatrice was not there to see it? Salai protested. Had Leonardo not heard that Isabella had sent fish from Lake Garda to the French king? Had he no sense of loyalty to Beatrice? Did he not need to get to Florence quickly? Did he not? No, he did not. They went to Mantua.

Isabella was gracious. She played the lute and sang for Leonardo, and she listened attentively as he sang for her. She showed them around her castle. She had a whole suite of rooms with low ceilings and small doors, and these were for her dwarfs, some of whom she had bred herself. Her best of breed she trained and sent to her relatives when they were in need of cheering up. Salai remembered his first conversation with Beatrice when she had been expecting Matello. "*You are very well proportioned for a dwarf,*" she had said.

Isabella's favorite part of the castle was her Studio of

the Grotto. There she kept her richest harvest of works of art. As they moved from room to room they saw ivories and silver and crucifixes. There were many musical instruments, all designed to her musical scale as the rooms of the dwarfs had been scaled for them.

In one room off the main court there sat a clavichord, an instrument so beautiful that only Lorenzo da Pavia could have designed it. Salai walked over to it and saw that it was ebony inlaid with ivory and all around it were mottoes in Latin and Greek. "Why, Duchess Beatrice has one just like this!" Salai exclaimed.

"Had," Isabella corrected.

"Well, yes," Salai said. He didn't always remember that Beatrice was dead.

"I asked the French for it, and they had it sent here," she continued.

"You asked the conquerors of your sister's castle for a favor?"

"I was doing the clavichord a favor. Such a work of art deserves a long life. I didn't want the clavichord to meet the same fate as Master Leonardo's horse." Leonardo bowed politely in recognition of the compliment.

Salai said nothing more.

A few days later, Aura, Isabella's pet dog, was killed. Isabella and all her courtiers at Mantua were plunged into the deepest mourning. "He never left my side," she cried.

"He was the handsomest and most amusing little dog that was ever known."

He was also the stupidest, Salai thought. Aura had been killed falling off a cliff pursuing a larger dog.

Isabella cried all during supper the night of the fatal accident. She also sighed loud and a lot.

Aura was buried in a specially designed lead casket in Isabella's animal cemetery. Along with everyone else at court, Leonardo and Salai were implored to attend the funeral. At the service, famous poets from Ferrara and from as far away as Rome sang songs in Latin and Italian in praise of the chaste and noble Aura. Isabella commissioned Romano, the sculptor who had done a bust of Beatrice when she was a girl, to design Aura's tombstone.

Salai did not know whether to laugh or to be outraged. He chose laughter.

Besides the clavichord, Isabella had also claimed the poets, the musicians and the agents who had hunted Italy for antiques for Beatrice. All were now in the service of Isabella. And Salai knew that Isabella would not rest until she had acquired Leonardo da Vinci, too.

Salai became determined that Isabella should not add Leonardo to her collection. He knew that Leonardo would sell his services to whomever he chose. Leonardo would not regard himself as being disloyal to Beatrice by being loyal to Isabella. Leonardo knew no loyalty save that of his own genius. And he could not be approached on the basis of sentiment any more than he could on the basis of loyalty. Leonardo regarded himself above such common feelings. Isabella herself would have to drive Leonardo out of Mantua. And Salai would have to drive Isabella to that.

"Dear Duchess Isabella," he said, "Master Leonardo has often expressed regret that you have ceased asking him to do your portrait. I know him well, and he is too shy to remind you himself. You are aware, of course, that he never painted Beatrice, your sister of blessed memory. I think her looks were too dark and not nobly formed. Frankly, one would have to say that she did not inspire the master. I am sure that is the reason he never committed her face to canvas. How otherwise can you explain that he painted both of the other women loved by Il Moro?" Salai then lowered his voice and said confidentially, "I'm referring, of course, to Cecilia Gallerani and Lucrezia Crivelli."

Isabella took the bait. She would make up for Leonardo's shyness. She flirted and cajoled. Leonardo, knowing that he was a guest in the house of the aristocracy, obliged. He did a sketch of Isabella in charcoal.

Leonardo's drawing was not kind; it was honest. He chose to draw Isabella's profile, her hair loose about her shoulders. He showed the beginnings of her double chin and the lumpy line of her shoulders and—unkindest stroke

—he showed her eyes. Eyes that betrayed no amusement, eyes that showed self-interest. Salai thought that Leonardo's drawing, a silent editorial, might make an end of the lady's begging for a portrait.

But it did not.

Isabella was too greedy. She felt now that she was closer than ever to two of her life goals, and the two would be rolled into one. Not only would she have some work from the hand of Leonardo da Vinci, she would also have the portrait she had longed for. A bargain. Isabella would not give up. Leonardo, who had so accurately drawn those eyes, should have known that, and part of him did. But the silent, lonely part of him, the part of him that wanted acceptance, did not.

Morning, noon and night Isabella nagged. Leonardo who had little patience with the actual act of painting, Leonardo who would assign such work to his apprentices whenever he could, this Leonardo put her off. Day after day she proposed, and day after day he postponed.

She never raised her voice. She never demanded. She never commanded. She never suggested that Leonardo owed her something in return for her hospitality. She merely talked and talked and talked. Salai smiled as he remembered *Isabellasays*. No one who came to the castle for a stay longer than five minutes could escape being shown the drawing. "Leonardo," she would announce, "will soon add color to this pale, pale cheek." She would smile at her audience and at Leonardo.

Leonardo would smile back.

Salai saw that as Isabella's smile became wider, Leonardo's became weaker. He knew that they would soon leave for Venice.

They did.

THEY SPENT a month in Venice, finally arriving in Florence in the spring of the year of the new century. It was Leonardo's first visit home in seventeen years and Salai's first visit ever.

Florence was a republic; there was no Duke of Florence as there had been in Milan and Mantua and Venice. There was no court around which the life of arts centered. There were many rich men who sponsored the arts; there were many powerful businessmen in love with scholarship and music and art. And they welcomed Leonardo with commissions and civic duties. He was appointed to a committee to decide where to place the statue of David that the young sculptor Michelangelo had completed for the city of Florence; the town fathers, not a duke, had commissioned him to do it. And the town fathers commissioned Leonardo to paint a battle scene on one wall of the City Hall, and they commissioned Michelangelo to do one on the wall opposite.

Secretive, tall, handsome, elegantly dressed Leonardo found nothing to like in the short, homely, unkempt, quick-tongued Michelangelo. And Michelangelo's wit found an easy target in the touchy, sensitive son returned home. The two giants of art and engineering did not get along.

Beatrice had been right: Leonardo had a thin skin indeed. He was easily deflated. That great mound of talent and intellect, as she had called him, stayed aloft on pride. Actually, Salai hated to see anyone best his master. He himself had little more respect for learning now that he was living among the sages of Florence than he had had when he was visiting among the scholars of Pavia. But he had learned to hold his tongue; he had also learned to use it well. At twenty he still did for the master what he had done when he was half that age. But now he did it consciously and conscientiously. After an evening among the famous of Florence, Salai often found himself pumping the master back up, making remarks that were both witty and wild and causing the master to laugh. Leonardo could never laugh at himself, but he could laugh at this irreverent young friend, this Salai who was almost part of himself.

Each new day was an enemy to Leonardo; he could not be satisfied with yesterday's well-done work. When he received the commission to paint the battle scene on the wall of the City Hall, he was not content that his work be his best; it had to be better than Michelangelo's. It had to be astounding. He worked on some new formulas for paints and a different method for drying them, and the whole of his work melted, melted and oozed down the wall. It was as Beatrice had said. The work had no proper sense of unimportance. The audience, the subject and the patron were all too important. Too important. Serious. Too serious. Leonardo had tried too hard.

Florence was a city in love with art. The Florentines would go anywhere, suffer any discomfort to partake of something new in art. They were fevered with culture. When Leonardo did the cartoon of an altarpiece for the Servite brothers, Salai invited some merchants in to see the work. Those merchants passed along word that in the studio of Leonardo da Vinci was a sight not to be missed. Soon everyone wanted to look. On the days that followed, men and women, young and old, crowded into the room where Salai displayed the cartoon. Salai charged admission. Those few merchants who had first been invited had no idea that they had been bait; they had felt privileged.

Salai closed the door of the studio to visitors when he received word that the master was returning from his retreat in the hills. Leonardo had once again seriously taken up his studies of flight.

Salai also enjoyed arranging audiences for the merchants who came to Florence. Everyone got something. The merchant got anecdotes to return home with. Leonardo got bellows for his pride, and Salai got money for his efforts. Dukes and princes would tell their courts how the master had looked, how softly he had spoken, and how he had promised them (in all confidence) that as soon as he had a gap in his schedule he would do their portrait. Leonardo promised them all. He always promised. He simply never delivered.

It was Isabella who would not be easily put off. She was more determined than ever to have her portrait done. She had more reason for hope than the others. Leonardo's promise to her was already half fulfilled. She wrote to Cecilia Gallerani and asked that lady, her sister's rival, to please send her the portrait that the master had done. What she saw made her even more anxious to have herself immortalized. She began a campaign that was to last for three years. It began with letters:

M. Leonardo,—Hearing that you are settled at Florence, we have begun to hope that our cherished desire to obtain a work by your hand may at length be realized. When you were in this city and drew our portrait in carbon, you promised us that you would some day paint it in colors. If you will consent to gratify this our great desire, remember that apart from the payment which you shall fix yourself, we shall remain so deeply obliged to you that our sole desire will be to do what you wish, and from this time forth we are ready to do your service and pleasure.

M. Leonardo,—You sent word by Messer Angelo some time ago that you would gladly satisfy my great desire. But the large number of orders which you receive make me fear lest you have forgotten mine. I have, therefore, thought it well to write these few words, begging you to paint this little figure by way of recreation when you are tired.

As soon as Isabella discovered that Leonardo found letters easy things to ignore, she hired Brother Pietro to deliver her messages and to keep Leonardo's promise ever before his eyes. This left Brother Pietro in the position of composing good letters out of poor excuses.

Most illustrious and excellent Lady,—
From what I hear, Leonardo's manner of life is very changeable and uncertain so that he seems to live for the day only. Since he has been in Florence, he has made only one sketch—a cartoon—and this sketch is not yet finished. He has done nothing else, excepting that two of his apprentices are painting portraits to which he sometimes adds a few touches. He is working hard at geometry, and is quite tired of painting.

Most illustrious and excellent Lady,—
I have succeeded in learning the painter Leonardo's inten-
tions by means of his pupil Salai. In truth his mathe-
matical experiments have absorbed his thoughts so entirely that he cannot bear the sight of a paintbrush. If he
can, as he hopes, end his engagement with the King of
France without displeasing him by the end of a month at
the latest, he would rather serve Your Excellency than
any other person in the world.

Most illustrious Madonna,—
I am glad to tell you that a pupil of Leonardo da Vinci,
Salai by name, young in years but very talented, has a
great wish to do some gallant thing for Your Excellency.
So if you desire a little picture, or anything else from him,
you have only to tell me the price you are ready to give,
and I will see that you are pleased.

Her Excellency, the Most illustrious Madonna, did not
accept Salai's offer.

SALAI was delighted with Isabella's pleas and letters. He would glady have paid both postage and entertainment tax on them. Many people who came to the studio had news of Isabella. Nothing in the reports he received convinced Salai to like her any better. He was pleased that Leonardo was busy with church commissions and geometry and the study of flight. There was small chance that he would find time to finish Isabella's portrait. Sooner or later she would come to realize that here was one prize that was just out of range of her jeweled pink fingers. Three years had passed since they had left Mantua, and still Leonardo had not produced the finished work. And still Isabella persisted. Perhaps in another three years she would know. Salai would like some way, some way other than letters and other than waiting, for her to realize that a work from Leonardo's hand would ever ever be beyond her grasp. Some way that would be final, polite and a little bit mean.

One day as Salai was quietly working in the studio, touching up the background for a study of Mary and the infant Jesus, a merchant appeared at the door of the workroom. Leonardo was at his country home studying the flow of rivers and the flight of birds, and Salai knew that this man's visit would not be profitable. He was a Florentine. Every now and then Salai could extract a few coins from some out-of-town merchant who would be content to tell people back home that he had visited the studio of Leonardo da Vinci, neglecting to add that Leonardo was not there at the time. But this man would not pay for half a package. Salai had no particular reason to be polite to him, but he had acquired a habit of good manners.

"Hello, there," he said. "What can I do for you?"

"I—ah—would like to see the—ah—maestro—ah— Maestro Leonardo."

"He is not in," Salai said. "Is there something I can do for you?"

"When will he—ah—return?"

"Maybe a day. Maybe a week. He is an artist, not a merchant. He does not keep regular hours," Salai said, his tone pleasant.

The man smiled and stepped inside the door. "Scusi," he said. "Me, I'm a merchant." He walked over to Salai's desk and laid a purse on it. Salai's expert eye calculated that it was large enough and fat enough to contain fifty ducats. "I—ah—would like Maestro Leonardo to do a—ah—painting for me."

Salai picked up the purse and tossed it lightly into the air. Yes, fifty ducats. He looked over at the man. "The King of France is waiting for a picture and the Duchess of Mantua has been waiting for over three years for him to finish hers. Both of them allow Master Leonardo to name his own price." He tossed the purse in the air again. "What makes you think that Master Leonardo will do a painting for you?"

The man held up a forefinger and gave it a small whirl. Then he aimed the finger at his chest. "I pay," he said, then whirled his finger again, pointing it at Salai, and added, "the maestro paints."

"I suppose," Salai continued, "that you have a good idea of what you want. A wall-sized painting of the Journey of the Magi with all the animals in the manger and all the stars in the heavens—"

"No," the merchant said, holding up his forefinger again. "*Scusi,* but with all—ah—respect to the maestro, I don't

—ah—want a journey." He retrieved the purse from Salai momentarily and then slapping it back down on the table said, "This money is for a—ah—portrait of my wife." He then turned and marched to the door, his back arched, his steps high and wide. He turned back to Salai momentarily and said "*Scusi*" again and stepped outside the door.

Salai was too amused to be angry. He laid his brush down. The merchant reentered, bringing with him a young woman about half his age.

The lady was embarrassed. She kept her head low as her husband led her into the room. Salai said hello, and the lady lifted her head and looked at Salai out of the corners of her eyes. Salai was unprepared for the look. It was two things: it was totally familiar, and it was totally strange. What was it? The smile? The look?

What was it?

He looked at her again. She was the same age as Beatrice would have been. That was it. She was the Beatrice he had known; that explained the familiar.

But she was a stranger, too. And then he realized: she was what Beatrice would have become.

This was a woman who knew that she was not pretty and who had learned to live with that knowledge. This was a woman whose acceptance of herself had made her beautiful in a deep and hidden way. A woman whose look told you that you were being sized by a measuring rod in her head; a measuring rod on which she alone had etched the units. A woman who knew how to give pleasure and how to give pain. A woman who knew how to endure. A woman of layers.

As soon as that thought came to him, Salai knew that he could persuade Leonardo to do it. He knew that there was something haunting about this lady's looks, something that only Leonardo could capture in paint.

She would be the portrait of Beatrice that he had never done. Leonardo would do this portrait because he wanted to and because Salai wanted him to. What an answer to Isabella. A perfect answer. That Leonardo should choose to paint the portrait of this woman, only a few steps above a peasant. He would pose her simply, in a simple dress, her hair loose. He would do for her everything that he had almost committed to Isabella, and Isabella would know for certain that Leonardo's sketch of her had been finished in the portrait of this other woman, this merchant's wife.

Salai leaned his head back and looked at her. What a good job Leonardo would do. And he would do it alone; no apprentice's hand would touch it. It would be a better job than he had done of Cecilia or Lucrezia or than he could ever do of Isabella. There would be no court rules to follow, no jewelry to obey. It would be Beatrice, but better. Because this lady would be the one unimportant element, the one importantly unserious element, the one wild thing that Beatrice had said that Leonardo always needed to make his work great. By urging Leonardo to do it, he would be fulfilling the responsibility Beatrice had urged on him.

Salai tossed the sack of coins into the air. "I might get the master to do your wife's portrait after all," he said. He put the purse in his drawer and turned toward the lady. She met his look once again. Still looking at her, Salai asked the merchant, "And what, sir, is your lady's name?"

The merchant clicked his heels, smiled, bowed slightly and with a sweep of his hand answered, "I present to you my—ah—my newest wife, Madonna Lisa. Me? I'm Mr. Giaconda."

Drawing of old man and youth (possibly Salai).

Leonardo, self portrait.

*Ludovico Sforza, detail from the Sforza Altarpiece
by the Maestro della Pala Sforzesco.*

COURTESY ALINARI-ART REFERENCE BUREAU.

Cecilia Gallerani.

DIVAE

Beatrice d'Este—bust by Gian Cristoforo Romano.

Sketch of Isabella d'Este.

COURTESY ALINARI-ART REFERENCE BUREAU.

The Star of Bethlehem and other plants.

The Last Supper. COURTESY ALINARI-ART REFERENCE BUREAU.